Tell Him About It

HOLLY KINSELLA

CONTENTS

"To be beloved is all I need,
And whom I love, I love indeed."
S.T. Coleridge.

"I thought I'd put the sparkle back into our relationship," Simon Keegan said charmingly as Sara Sharpe opened the box from Selfridge's and the sapphire earrings glinted in the candlelight. Sara's face lit up and her gasp voiced her gratitude and happiness. It could be argued however that some of her happiness and gratitude was down to the box not containing an engagement ring. Sara began to blush as she noticed how her reaction had turned a number of heads in the Mayfair restaurant.

Simon smiled at her, although Sara sensed just as much self-satisfaction as affection in his smirk. But perhaps she was being a little unfair in such a judgement.

Sara had met Simon around six months ago at a book launch she had helped arrange, as a publicity assistant for one of her authors. After working the room for most of the evening, carrying a tray of canapés in one hand and a bottle of wine in the other (whilst constantly blowing her fringe out of her eyes as she did so), Sara was able to draw breath and speak to one or two of the guests in earnest. The author introduced Simon as being a friend from their days at Oxford. He was well dressed and well mannered. He complimented her on her outfit – a red floral tea dress that she had recently bought in a House of Fraser sale – which brought a smile to her face. And then he kindly poured her a glass of wine and brought a tray of canapés over, which made her smile even more.

"You seem to forever be looking after someone else this evening. It's high time someone looked after you."

"Thank you."

She immediately enjoyed his company. He took in what she was saying, as opposed to just taking in the lines of her figure. At the end of the evening he also generously offered to pay the bar tab for the party.

"Now let's not have our first argument – let's save that for when we chat about religion or politics – but I'd like to pay for the drinks this evening Sara."

"No, you mustn't. My publishers have agreed to pay."

"No, I insist. Without me leaning over to copy the essays of our clever author friend over there I would have never have graduated. I'd like to do something nice for him to celebrate the publication of the book."

Simon won the argument and picked up the drinks bill. Sara was nervous about telling her publicity director, Margaret Duvall, about accepting payment from someone else the next day but, for once, her boss praised her. "Darling, whatever dress you wore to the event wear it to the next one. See what happens when you show some leg." Sara realised that with the budget freed up from not paying for the party Margaret Duvall (or *Cruella* as she nicknamed her) could afford to take even more people out for long lunches in Kensington.

"Can I send you a book as a thank you?" Sara asked Simon at the end of the night.

"Unfortunately I don't have time to read books. But I'd like to make time to take you out to dinner Sara. I've the good sense and taste to want to get to know you more."

They dated and she got to know him more too. He worked as a financial consultant. Simon was good looking and clean cut, as much as he tried to occasionally give himself the swagger of a "city boy" and "mockney". He was decent and smart, if a little too po-faced sometimes. He was also hardworking, but perhaps too much so. She half-joked to her flatmate, Rosie, that there were three in the relationship – him, her and his Blackberry.

He invited her to expensive restaurants and exclusive parties. Although Sara had spent time in that world before when she had been a model (and had dated an actor and also a top football agent) she pretended to be wowed and impressed. She was soon spending more time with him than anyone else. They went away for the weekend together, to Venice and then to New York. She asked him if he wanted to travel to the Lake District for a week (she'd always wanted to go since reading Wordsworth and Coleridge at university) but he said that he couldn't get the time off work.

Sara was soon spending a large portion of her time at his apartment in Baron's Court. She began to care about him. He had recently sent her a text message saying "*I love you*". It had been late at night. He had no doubt had a drink, Sara thought, and she hoped that he thought she wasn't replying because she had fallen asleep. She met his parents several times. Sara liked Simon's mother, Valerie. She was less impressed with his father, Gordon, however. He was a reactionary Tory who considered that it should be a woman's ambition in life to become a "Domestic Goddess". Rosie and other friends – and her own family who had met and liked Simon – had started to ask of late whether she was going to get engaged. "You make a good couple," her mother had said.

Good, but not great.

Something was missing. Simon had joked that he wanted to put the sparkle back into their relationship, but how much was he being serious too? And had the sparkle ever been there in the first place? Was she still with him because he had just become a habit, part of her routine? But was he not a good habit? He wasn't overly vain or selfish – like a number of her ex-boyfriends. But yet, increasingly, Sara realised that he wasn't overly fun or selfless either. She felt safe with him, but didn't she also occasionally feel bored when in his company? She sometimes felt like she was just there to be the trophy ex-model girlfriend when she was with him. But she liked it when she made him happy. Was she experiencing a fear of commitment, or was she just fearful of committing to him? Was there something wrong with Simon, or something wrong with her? Rosie had half-jokingly said the previous evening how she was doomed if she wanted to find Mr Perfect.

"Mr Perfect is also Mr No One," she added, her arm disappearing down the tube of crisps to fish out the last one. Rosie was her oldest friend – a sarcastic and sweet-natured journalist, who worked for their local newspaper.

"I'm not looking for somebody who's perfect. I'm just looking for someone who can stop my heart, or start it. Someone who can make me laugh and who has a love of Jane Austen, Samuel Taylor Coleridge, Billy Joel and muffins for breakfast," Sara had half-jokingly replied, her arm disappearing behind the fridge door, as she grabbed another bottle of wine.

But tonight was going to be the night, Sara thought, as she sat in the taxi on the way to the restaurant. They needed to talk... but what should they talk about? Should she talk about ending things, or possibly starting a life together? What did Simon want? Did she even know what *she* wanted? The gift of the earrings had rendered Sara even more speechless and hesitant about confronting the two dozen questions she had often asked herself of late.

"They're lovely. You're lovely," she finally said.

What Sara was unable to say, however, were the words "I love you."

2.

Simon asked her – again – to stay the night with him just before their desserts were served. Sara had already explained that she had some work to catch up on that evening, due to having to meet a new author the next day. The varnished smile fell from his face and he pursed his lips in disappointment. He tried again just after paying the bill.

"Please, I could use the company tonight babe. I've had a long week," he said, reaching over the table and lacing his fingers into hers.

Sara had believed him for the first few times when he wore a puppy-dog expression and said that he needed company during the night. But what he really wanted was sex. She didn't mind though, most of the time. He was a good lover.

Good, but not great.

Sara repeated that she had some important work to do, although Simon seldom understood or cared when she spoke about her work nowadays. Managing financial portfolios and pension funds was important, he considered. Arranging a book signing or an author interview with the *Yorkshire Post* wasn't. Aside from when she spoke about how much money certain authors received in advances he often had a disinterested look on his face, or changed the subject, when talk of publishing came up. He used his tablet for checking the football scores, or playing a game, rather than reading, she had noticed.

Simon coiled his arm around Sara and kissed her, amorously, when they left the restaurant. It was a sultry June evening. The brightest stars shone through the hazy London sky. Shepherd Market was lively with half-drunk hedge fund managers and curious (or lost) tourists. Smokers lined the pavement outside the bars and restaurants. Half the men wore Italian or Savile Row suits, whilst the other half wore designer jeans with Ralf Lauren polo shirts. The women wore smart business suits, or skimpy summer tops and short skirts (or less). Cab drivers rolled their eyes as middle-aged men and their secretaries stumbled into the back seats of their taxis.

"You really do look beautiful tonight," Simon suddenly remarked, stopping to admire his girlfriend. Behind the sweetness in his voice though was horniness, Sara thought. They were approaching Green Park, where they would catch cabs in opposite directions. The compliment and look in his eye was borne more from desperation than genuine affection, as he tried for the last time to get her to stay the night with him.

Simon had been right though. Sara did look beautiful. A blonde bob framed a pretty face and sun-kissed complexion. Her blue eyes shone with intelligence, kindness and humour. She wore make-up, but not much. She was naturally beautiful – and donning too much make-up reminded her of the rituals and regimes of when she was a fashion model in her teens. Even in flats Sara was tall – and when she wore heels it unfortunately gave men the perfect excuse to stare at her breasts at their eye level.

In regards to her modelling career Sara retired herself years ago. The money was good, but her heart wasn't in it.

"You have the cheek bones my dear, but not the determination to make it to the top," one agent had said to her.

The industry wanted to possess her, body and soul. There was an oppressive, nasty culture of needing to constantly diet. "There are plenty of Estonian girls I can get to lose the weight – and gain the look – if you won't," she was told on more than one occasion by a photographer or someone in a fashion house. Sara couldn't remember the amount of times she had been pinched by a dresser and then told to "lose it". Drugs were freely given out at parties, partly to make guests dependant on the scene – and partly girls were encouraged to take (some) drugs because they were "wonderful appetite suppressants". Photographers were often misogynistic, whether gay or straight, male or female. Modelling agencies, either subtly or blatantly, threatened models with dropping them if they did not accept every job. The industry was far from all glamour. There was a culture of sadism, rather than a sorority, between the models themselves which Sara didn't like. Everyone smiled when in front of someone, but then bitched about them as soon as their back was turned – as if to behave in any other way would be unnatural.

With the money Sara made from modelling she put herself through university and bought a two bedroom flat in Clapham. She loved reading and books – and wishing to write a book one day herself she decided she wanted to work in publishing. She gained an internship with Bradley House, a major publisher based in Hammersmith. Sara impressed the publicity department enough for them to give her a temporary position covering for someone on maternity leave. They soon took her on permanently as a publicity assistant for their commercial fiction list. Although Sara neither liked nor respected her boss she did enjoy her job. She met lots of interesting people and was pleased when certain books took off, or when she arranged a publicity coup. Most, though certainly not all, of the authors she worked with were nice and grateful for the extra hours she put in. It wasn't just Simon who worked hard.

When Simon realised that he wasn't going to get his way and convince Sara to stay the night he grew a little sullen – and pouted. They kissed each other good night however and Sara flagged down a taxi to take her home.

She pulled out her phone and tried to make inroads into her inbox during the journey back to Clapham. An author had thanked her for a successful event she had arranged for him at a literary festival. A creative writing magazine had got back to her to say that they would like to profile a crime writer she looked after. Sara rolled her eyes though upon reading an email from her boss, Cruella Duvall.

Sara, be a darling and pick up my dry cleaning tomorrow. I've got a busy morning at the hairdresser's and I won't have time. Thanks, M.

Sara also received a message from a new author she was about to work with, confirming their meeting for tomorrow. Adam Cooper was a bestselling military thriller writer. He had been called "the thinking man's Andy McNab," which was more than a little unfair on Andy McNab and whoever had ghost written his books. Sara had inherited the publicity campaign from a colleague who had recently left the company to go travelling. Although a *Sunday Times* Top Ten author Adam Cooper had become more famous recently for having married the socialite celebrity, Victoria Glass. Or rather his name had been in the papers of late for having divorced her. Sara had checked out the latest gossip on the pair that morning. She was forever being photographed by the paparazzi coming out of parties and restaurants, with a different date each time (a rugby player, actor, TV presenter, property tycoon). She had also given a number of interviews on daytime television, hinting that she had tried her best with the marriage but it had failed due to her husband's drinking and affairs. Newspapers always reported that Adam Cooper was unable to comment in reply to his wife's allegations.

Sara spent the rest of the evening reading Adam Cooper's new book, *Hidden Agenda*.

3.

"You need to use it, without letting Cooper know you're doing so," Margaret Duvall remarked, perching herself on the desk. She anxiously tapped her foot, her body craving another cigarette. She wore a close-fitting blood red dress which showed off her long, tanned (orange) legs to Julian Smythe, Adam Cooper's editor. Margaret Duvall loved flirting with younger men – nearly as much as she liked bullying younger women. She was a faded beauty, whose traits of bitterness and incompetence were still in bloom, Sara mused.

"But I don't want to lie, either to the author or my contacts," Sara replied, sitting before them like a pupil who had been called into the headmaster's office. The pair had asked her to spread the word to feature journalists and TV and radio that Cooper would talk about his marriage in exchange for talking about the new book – although the author had already given express instructions that he didn't want to be interviewed about his ex-wife.

"Darling, if you're uncomfortable with lying, then why did you ever choose to become a publicist?" the publicity director posited, only half joking, in her shrill voice.

Julian Smythe gave off a conspiratorial chuckle, flicking his long fringe out of his eyes as he did so. Many of the women in the office found the editor attractive and charming, although Sara begged to differ. He was average height, average build – indeed he was average in a remarkable number of ways, she thought. He was well groomed, well spoken and had attended Eton. Unfortunately he came away from the school with a sense of entitlement, rather than a good education. Julian had made a clumsy pass at her at the Christmas party six months ago.

"Let's just have this one night Sara. We've both wanted this for a while. I'll help you get a job in editorial... I want to un-wrap you like a Christmas present... Just one night. It'll mean nothing," he had argued, or rather drunkenly pleaded.

"It may not mean 'nothing' to your wife though," Sara had wryly replied – extricating herself from the awkward scene. Julian had seldom been amiable or professionally supportive since the embarrassing encounter, but Sara was compensated by the fact that the arrogant creep mainly kept his distance now. There also seemed to be plenty of other young women in the office who he, sometimes quite literally, licked his lips over.

The plants in his office were as artificial as his smile. Although the screen saver on the monitor was the original cover of *The Great Gatsby* Sara had, on more than one occasion, seen porn on his computer. Julian Smythe had originally secured his job in publishing, after graduating from Exeter University, through being the best friend of the son of the company's old managing director. The publishing industry is more incestuous than Wales (or Texas) in regards to the nepotism and cronyism which serves as its recruitment policy (indeed Bradley House's idea of ethnic diversity was to employ the occasional white South African as a temporary receptionist). The gene pool of labour was as shallow as Julian Smythe. Sara didn't rate his judgement or productivity as an editor either. He had recently published a string of flops, overpaying in terms of advances and not shaping books correctly.

"Fucking supermarkets. They've buried the book before it's even published. Bloody plebs. They took on his last two books, why haven't they picked this one up?" Julian had bemoaned the other week, after hearing about the low pre-orders for one of his crime writers. The following day however, when the author and his agent had come in for a meeting, he had argued that "Waterstones can still break a book... and there's always WH Smith's Travel... and a buyer at an independent chain says he really likes the cover and may order in a few extra copies... but we cannot now justify a tube advert campaign... although it looks like we may be able to include you on a panel event at a Crime Festival..."

The smarmy editor thought that he had glossed over things well in the meeting. The rest of the people in the room thought differently however.

Thankfully, for Julian, he still looked after two bestselling authors – who the company directors knew were loyal to Smythe and would walk if Bradley House sacked the editor. One of the bestselling authors played in Julian's cricket team and the other was his second cousin. Julian's other bankable writer though was Adam Cooper and the publishers had just tabled an offer to sign up his next three books. Cooper and his agent had said that they would wait and see how the latest release performed before committing to further titles. Hence Sara had been called into the office and told to perform – and weight her time towards promoting *Hidden Agenda,* to the point of ignoring the other writers in her care for the month. An intern could just stuff review copies of their books into jiffy bags to an out-dated mailing list – and that would serve as their publicity campaign.

"So do you understand what you've got to do?" Margaret Duvall said, tapping her feet with even greater urgency. "Devote all of your time to Cooper. Promise the press they can have an exclusive interview with him about Victoria Glass if they plug the book. But make sure Cooper doesn't find out. He'll thank us in the end when we generate extra sales. He just doesn't know what's best for him at the moment. And show some leg while you're with him. If reports from his wife are true, he fancies himself as a ladies' man. We've already arranged some events around the country so you'll have a week to impress him and convince him that we're still the right home for his books."

Julian Smythe nodded in agreement and smiled as the senior publicist spoke, glancing both at her legs and then Sara's breasts as he did so. Sara felt uncomfortable, in regards to both her instructions and the leer on the editor's face, but she nodded her head to convey she understood. She knew she was being double-teamed and bullied. She knew that she was being set up for blame should Cooper not sign another contract. She knew that, sooner or later, the author would find out about the deception – or her press contacts would think less of her when they broached the subject of Cooper's ex-wife to him and he remained silent. But what could she say, or do?

Sara sighed as she sat back down at her desk. The colour – and life – had drained out of her face. Her friend and fellow publicist, Polly (Julian creepily nicknamed her "Pretty Polly"), asked if she was feeling okay. Sara forced a smile and nodded, unconvincingly, whilst saying she was fine. Sara sighed again, however, after seeing how her inbox had filled up once more during the time that she had been in the meeting. Most of the emails were from a variety of authors (some needy, some grateful, some businesslike, some conceited). Before attempting the Sisyphean task of trying to clear her messages – she did not have the heart to completely ignore them – Sara decided to take her tea break. She needed a caffeine fix and wanted a shoulder to cry on in regards to the recent meeting. As she walked through the open plan office Sara witnessed others on their breaks, or "working". A number were on their personal Facebook accounts or watching YouTube – or sending out messages about the latest moral outrage trending on twitter, or reacting to the latest episode of a faddish reality TV show. Others did their nails or gossiped (the productive people were able to do both at the same time). To be fair though, one or two people were genuinely hard at work, Sara noticed. Everyone blamed eBooks and Amazon for revenues being down, but there was an elephant in the room when they made that case – and the elephant was complacency.

Sara found a quiet spot outside of her building. She knew that Rosie would be busy this time of day so she called Simon. The call went to voicemail (he seldom answered his phone) but he quickly sent an email via his Blackberry as compensation.

All well babe? xx

Yes – and no. Just could use someone to talk to. Not having the greatest day at work.

Sorry, can't talk right now. Just about to have a lunch meeting with some clients. Don't fret about work tho'. Think happy thoughts. Treat yourself to a pastry and keep your spirits – and serotonin levels – up. Think about your recent pay rise and how much more gorgeous and sexy you are, compared to your gnarled and scatty bitch of a boss. Xx

Can we talk, just for two minutes? Just want to hear your voice. xx

But he failed to reply.

4.

Sara sat in the coffee shop across the road from her building and looked at her watch again. Adam Cooper was fifteen minutes late. She was already anxious about the meeting, given his reputation for drinking and womanising. She also still felt uncomfortable about her task of approaching the press and pitching that Cooper would talk about his failed marriage against his wishes. Sara had dealt with authors who had big egos, or flirted with her and thought they were God's gift to women before – she could (just about) handle that. But she had never actively betrayed someone like she had been asked to do in regards to Adam Cooper. The waiting only made it worse.

She recognised her author from his book jacket photo as he walked through the door. Adam scanned the room, not knowing what his publicist looked like. Sara smiled and waved at him. He was dressed casually in a navy blue polo shirt, jeans and well worn boots. He was unshaven and his short-ish brown crop of hair was unkempt. His eyes were red-rimmed with drink, or a lack of sleep. His face seemed weathered, but filled with good humour too. In some ways he appeared older than he was, but his boyish smile could then make him seem younger than his thirty-three years. As Adam thrust out his hand to shake Sara's she noticed a pale white mark on his tanned wedding band finger from where he had recently removed his ring.

"Sorry for being late. Do you mind if we go somewhere else for our meeting? There's a pub next door. I'm not really one for coffee shops, not because of their policy towards avoiding paying tax but I can't stand the inane conversation and self-satisfied people in them. At least when people talk bollocks in a pub they've the excuse that they've had a drink."

Sara noticed that his South London accent came through when Cooper swore. When she read up on him she discovered that the author was originally brought up in Eltham, the son of a bricklayer and dinner lady. His formal education was minimal (a few critics even insinuated that his books must have been ghost written, as they believed that no one without a university education, like theirs, could have written them). Cooper had joined the army at an early age but left after his first tour of Afghanistan. His first book, a military thriller set in Helmand, was an instant bestseller and he had written half a dozen books since. Sara offered her author a look of disapproval on his suggestion that they go to the pub, as she thought it inappropriate, but he pretended not to notice and turned to head back out of the overly trendy, over priced coffee shop.

Sara arched her eyebrow a little on entering the slightly less than trendy public house, *The Duke of Marlborough*. She arched it even more when she had to brush crumbs of food off her seat before she sat down – as she also noticed a trio of regulars at the bar raise their eyebrows in appreciation at the former fashion model.

"Would you like a drink?" Adam asked. A twinkle lit up his expression as soon as he entered the pub, Sara couldn't help but observe.

"Just a mineral water will be fine," she replied.

Adam offered his prim publicist a slight look of disapproval – he thought it inappropriate not to order a proper drink – but Sara pretended not to notice and turned to fish around in her handbag for her notes on the publicity schedule. She watched, however, as Adam went to the bar and made the (bottle) blonde barmaid laugh, as he bought her a drink also.

When Adam sat back down Sara ran through the publicity itinerary – and pitch list – that she was working on. He was due to take part in a number of signings and book talks, in and outside London, over the coming week. He was also set to give a few interviews via phone and email – and write a couple of short articles for crime and military magazines. When they returned from their short tour there would be a publication dinner.

Adam nodded, shrugged and replied that all was fine in regards to what Sara had said. He wore a distracted, dislocated, look on his face while she spoke however. He seemed to only wake from his trance when the barmaid came over to collect his empty glass and serve him another drink. When Sara finished running through her notes she asked if Adam had any questions.

"Not really. Let's just take things one day at a time. I should apologise beforehand Sara that I may be dragging you into a media circus, with my ex-wife as the ringmaster and me walking the tightrope, or rather being a clown.

Journalists may well approach you with a token interest in the book and then ask about Victoria. I don't really want to comment and put my private life, or hers, in the spotlight. The press are not good at taking no for an answer, but they're going to have to learn to do so in this instance. Life has had its pound of flesh out of me. There's nothing left for the tabloids."

Adam spoke in a calm, reasonable way but there was a wounded look on his face. For a moment or two she felt sorry for him – but then remembered his wife's side of the story, his drinking and womanising – which she had witnessed evidence of within ten minutes of meeting him. After a short pause however, Adam Cooper snapped out of whatever mood he was in.

"Yet thanks to the tabloids and various websites you may know everything you need to know about me. But tell me more about yourself Sara," he remarked, draining the remainder of his pint and then turning to catch the eye of the smiling barmaid again. It struck Sara that he hadn't known the woman for more than thirty minutes and they acted like they were old friends.

"What would you like to know?" she replied, a little taken aback due to the fact that most authors were far fonder of talking about themselves.

"Some say that we are what we read, so tell me about a couple of books you've read recently, although feel free to leave out the ones you've been obliged to read for your work, including mine."

She often spoke to Rosie about the books she read (in regards to people in work they usually only discussed the titles the publishing house released; it never ceased to surprise Sara too just how little some people read, whilst supposedly trying to carve out a career in publishing). And Simon didn't even pretend to read, or be interested in what Sara was reading, nowadays.

"Just for fun I've been re-reading Jilly Cooper's early, short romance novels. Before she started writing bonkbusters. Her first books are more about love, than sex. The two are not one and the same."

"No. Though it's much nicer when they share the same bed."

Sara didn't quite know whether to laugh or blush, so she did both. They continued to chat about books, with the conversation spiralling off into different directions. Part of her wanted to act professionally or even coldly towards the author. Before she met him she had predicted that he would be self-obsessed, macho and come on to her – like a number of other soldiers or foreign correspondents turned novelists she had encountered. But he seemed to be healthily self-deprecating, polite and normal (which made him special in a sense, in terms of novelists).

"And so have you read anything else? You must also tell me if I'm eating too much into your time."

"No, it's fine," Sara replied, thinking how she was doing what she had been asked to. Namely look after her author. Besides, she was starting to enjoy herself. "While I was at university I studied Romantic poetry, so I've just read the newly published biography of Byron. I've got quite eclectic tastes. Are you familiar with Byron?" Sara asked, expecting the negative reply that she always received. But Adam Cooper, she was learning, was different.

"In secret we met
In silence I grieve -
That thy heart could forget,
Thy spirit deceive.
And if I should meet thee
After these long years,
How should I greet thee?-
With silence and tears."

Sara's eyes widened, in shock as much as pleasure. She sat, her mouth agape, as if an echo of Byron himself was sitting across the table. Such had been the sadness – and tenderness – in his voice when reciting the lines that Sara imagined that Adam had pictured her as a lost love, or his ex-wife? Melancholy infected his already dark eyes. He looked endearingly vulnerable after quoting the lines, she considered.

"I read a fair bit of poetry in my youth too. The barmaids love it," Adam wryly remarked, regaining his composure, politely leaving out the lesson for Sara that she shouldn't judge a book by its cover.

Sara was tempted to reply that former models and publicity assistants like it too, but she reined herself in just in time. Authors were not supposed to flirt with publicists – but publicists were definitely not supposed to flirt with authors, whether the said authors had become recently single or not.

"And what have you been reading, if you don't mind me asking?" Sara asked, genuinely curious.

"Well aside from reading the final draft of my divorce papers – and hundreds of tweets and abusive emails from devotees of my ex-wife – I've just finished re-reading *Pride & Prejudice*. I needed to bolster my faith in love and happy endings," Adam remarked wistfully. "But let's just hope that we have a happy ending in regards to book sales. Don't worry though, I'm not a prima donna. I don't expect you to be a miracle worker," Adam amiably said. "I'm not sure about me being a miracle worker either, but I am about to turn this water into a glass of wine. Would you like another drink too?"

They both smiled and Adam and Sara looked at each other – differently.

5.

Sara returned to the office after two large glasses of wine. Adam thanked her for all the work she had done and said he looked forward to their book tour together. She suffered a twinge of disappointment in him – and perhaps jealousy in regards to herself – when she watched Adam perch himself on a stool and chat to the barmaid as she left the pub to go back to work. Thankfully her boss was nowhere to be seen at the office. Polly explained that she had left early. *Cruella* had to prepare for an evening out, meeting up with some old school friends from Sherborne. Unfortunately Julian was still at work – and he offered the publicist a look of either dislike or desire through the glass partition of his corner office. Eton had helped turn him into a repressive one minute and a randy toad the next. He should go into politics.

"How was your meeting?" Polly asked eagerly, as Sara sat back down. Sara noticed the copy of a women's magazine on her friend's desk, with the page open at an article about Victoria Glass.

"Interesting," was the publicist's sphinx-like reply. Sara couldn't help but suppress a not so subtle grin as she still glowed from the recent drinks and company.

"Well do tell, what's he like?" Polly said, hoping to mine a nugget of celebrity gossip about the author's former wife from her friend.

"He can hold his drink, as well as a conversation," Sara remarked, as much to herself as to her colleague. Towards the end of their meeting together Sara had noted how she seemed tipsier than him – and he had drunk three times as much as her. Adam had charmingly shrugged and replied, "I was in the army. Drinking is part of basic training... Life can be hard. Drinking softens the edges." There had been both a wryness and a wistfulness to his tone. Adam Cooper was certainly more complex than the stock hero in his thrillers, Sara thought.

*

Sara's phone pinged with a text message as she put the key in the door to her flat in Clapham.

Sorry I couldn't talk earlier babe. Am out tonight entertaining clients, but chat tomorrow. Enjoy your evening without me (but not too much). Xxx

Although they had made a vague commitment to meet up and go for a drink or see a film Sara was fine to spend the night in. Rosie cooked her world famous (well, Clapham famous) chicken and mushroom risotto and Sara cleaned up afterwards as a thank you. The two friends then watched *Jerry Maguire* (again) whilst chatting idly about everything and nothing – and working their way through a bottle of white wine. When she heard the line in the film, "You complete me," Sara ironically felt hollow. She thought of Simon and their relationship. Sara realised she was somehow less than herself when with him, or not the person she wanted to be. Mrs Sara Keegan didn't sound or feel right. But she had now been with him for over six months. *Something* must have been working between them. Better to stick than bust was her mother's advice – especially after she had learned how much Simon earned.

"It's not about marrying Darcy, it's about making sure that you don't marry a Mr Collins or Wickham," Rosie had argued a month ago.

Before she went to bed to catch up on some reading Sara checked her emails and also Googled Victoria Glass. She was the daughter of Lord Mells, an aristocrat who had first made his money in property and then had recently increased his fortune through buying up land and selling it on to wind farm companies. For the past five years or so Victoria had been a darling of the tabloids – and broadsheets. Victoria Glass was stunningly beautiful, almost faultlessly so. She was tall, elegant, with classically sculptured features and glossy black hair. Magazines regularly cited her as a style icon. A website once conducted a study on the break-up of news on a given day and discovered that more column inches had been devoted to a dress Victoria Glass wore one evening than to coverage of the civil war in Syria. She had, over the years, modelled for a couple of couture fashion houses and Sara read that she was due to bring out her own perfume and evening wear collection. The paparazzi loved her and she always posed for the camera and would happily give a journalist a quote. Of course she also gave an interview about press intrusion and the need for new privacy laws. Sara clicked on a cynical blog article about the "Tabloid Courtesan" which said that she tipped photographers off when she was due to come out of a club or restaurant, or when her latest celebrity suitor would leave her house the morning after. Victoria also earned money through charging to attend launch parties or fashion shows, where she would sit in the front row next to the catwalk, chatting and laughing with similar tabloid courtesans like they were best friends.

There was little to read of in regards to Adam, although she did find a TV interview on YouTube the couple gave before they were married. They explained how they had met at a film premiere. Three months later they were engaged. The cynical blogger alleged that the engagement and marriage was just a promotional stunt, arranged by Victoria's agent. Yet as Sara watched the pair during their interview she was convinced of Victoria's devotion towards Adam. She wasn't that good an actress, Sara thought – though she read that Victoria had flown over to Hollywood for some screen tests during their marriage.

I can be myself when I'm with Adam... It's nice to spend an evening curled up on the sofa watching a movie in front of the TV with someone you love, rather than spending a night dolling yourself up and have a dozen cameras flash in your face outside a club... He's old-fashioned, honourable... You probably think, given our backgrounds, that we haven't got anything in common... But from that first night, during dinner after the film premiere, we knew we shared a sense of humour and a will to take care of one another in some way.

The marriage did not last long. Sara found a poignant quote from Victoria, from a brief interview she gave on the red carpet at an opening of a West End musical. "We worked better as friends than as husband and wife." Victoria was criticised by some for milking publicity from her divorce (whilst others argued that she should have been praised for her courage in walking away from her heavy drinking, unfaithful spouse). Both before and after the marriage Victoria was often labelled a "dumb blonde", despite her black hair. She was far from dumb though it seemed to Sara. She had studied History and Economics at LSE and had proved to be a shrewd networker and businesswoman. She read a feature in a magazine where one prominent feminist had called her "a media whore" whilst another had lauded her as being "an empowered 21st century woman". When Sara searched for Victoria Glass on twitter she, depressingly predictably, found swaths of messages by perverted men (and lesbians). There also seemed to be a virtual community of internet trolls that directed abuse and vitriol at her.

The messages on twitter reminded Sara of some of the comments she used to receive when she was a model. She sighed, turned off the computer and went to bed.

6.

In the morning Sara filled her time with every possible task, aside from calling the newspapers to pitch interviews with Adam about his ex-wife. She even welcomed being called into the monthly acquisitions meeting, at which the staff discussed various book proposals and submissions and whether they wanted to proceed with them or not. The meetings could sometimes be heated – or humorous – as a number of personalities and departments often clashed about what the company should be publishing. Books could be signed up sometimes due to which editor was having an affair with which member of the sales team (or books were not signed up due to said flings ending acrimoniously). Personal and political tastes more often than not eclipsed commercial sense. The marketing and sales team seldom championed literary fiction and serious non-fiction. Not because it couldn't sell, but because they neither read those types of books nor understood their appeal. "Old people" read military history; the grey pound (which in terms of a demographic was growing) was uninteresting or insignificant in the eyes of the twenty- and thirty-somethings in the marketing department. When one of the senior editors had called the younger generation "ahistorical" recently the marketing team looked blank-faced, until they looked the definition up on their iPads. Sara hoped that their publishing director would be at the meeting, so as to act as a headmaster when the schoolchildren got unruly and the bickering turned into full blown arguments.

Sara sat in the corner with Polly. She only really spoke when spoken to during such meetings. It was the sales, marketing and editorial teams who were most vocal during the discussions. It was as much a battle of egos, as opposed to ideas, as to which books were acquired she had long realised.

The publishing director, Martin Tweed, was indeed thankfully present and headed up the meeting, ably assisted by the senior editors for fiction (John Burke) and non-fiction (Charlotte Hurst). Various people from the sales department were also in attendance. They looked after key accounts, such as those with the supermarkets, Waterstones and Amazon. A dishevelled looking Eddie Woolly, who was the sales rep for independent bookshops, also sat himself in the corner, next to Polly. Nicotine stained fingertips scratched a half-grown beard. When he wasn't scowling at his colleagues during the meeting he was often yawning, to accentuate how bored he was. Sara liked Eddie though. He could be fun (when he was in a good mood) and he had a genuine encyclopaedic knowledge of what had been published in the past decade, having worked at Ottakar's for several years. Julian was present and sat with a handful of other editors and editorial assistants across the table from the significant players in the marketing and sales teams, ready to talk (argue) about any and everything. Most of the members of the marketing team, even the senior people, were younger than Sara. Their hair was filled with "product" and they checked their iPhones (mainly for Facebook updates) every two minutes. Most had a degree in marketing (from an old polytechnic) and most read no more than a dozen books a year, which was understandable given the amount of reality TV shows the women (girls) watched and given the amount of time the men (boys) spent playing Xbox.

There was already an air of tension in the room from previous meetings. A number of titles had either succeeded, or failed, over the past month. And in publishing success has many fathers, whilst failure is an orphan. Acquisition meetings for future titles were as much about previous books and previous arguments. Sara had now heard the sentiment "I told you so" expressed in more ways than she could remember. A conscious and unconscious fear that people could lose their job also stoked an already fractious atmosphere.

Everyone sat with a print out or tablet before them, containing info about the proposals to be discussed. First up was a biography of Unity Mitford, by the established historian Miranda Woodman, which Charlotte Hurst was hoping to sign-up.

"I've never heard of her," Troy Jones, a boisterous marketing assistant who was the nephew of the company's finance director, dismissively remarked – proud rather than ashamed of his ignorance of the Mitford sisters.

"The author is an established name, she will deliver a good book on time and if we can secure worldwide rights we'll be able to sell the book in US," Charlotte patiently replied, arguing for the acquisition to go ahead. Sara liked and respected Charlotte Hurst. She was fiercely intelligent and fiercely passionate about books. For decades she had been responsible for numerous bestselling and prizewinning works of History and Biography. The sales and marketing teams often made misogynistic or ageist jokes about Charlotte behind her back – but due to the loyalty of her stable of authors the sales and marketing teams knew that they couldn't pension her off quite yet.

"I'm not sure that the book will play to our strengths though," Chaz Connelly, the head of marketing who only ever showed enthusiasm for celebrity biographies and crime novels, said. Chaz was, unfortunately, Australian. He was forever internet shopping whilst at work and had a septum half burned out through a cocaine habit.

"Max, what do you think?" Martin Tweed asked, turning to his sales director, who was responsible for selling books into the supermarkets. Max Souness loved his job, wife and children though Sara suspected that, more than anything, Max Souness loved Max Souness. He was the youngest sales director in publishing and spoke with an authority which was borne from arrogance rather than experience. Yet he had worked hard at cultivating relationships with his key accounts and regularly persuaded the supermarkets to stock Bradley House titles. A trade magazine had named him as being the twelfth most powerful person in publishing.

Max waited for everyone to turn and look at him before pursing his lips and shaking his head, as if he were a doctor informing a family that the patient wouldn't make it. Eddie Woolly rolled his eyes and sighed, frustrated that Max Souness had again turned down what would likely be a well written – and profitable – book that the likes of Waterstones and independent bookshops could get behind. Yet he had faith that Charlotte could still rescue the project by talking to Martin Tweed in private at a later date.

The next book to be discussed was a crime novel, *Blood Work*, by a debut author, Christina Ponting. John Burke described the book as "a cross between Martina Cole and Peter James." Eddie Woolly sardonically chipped in that perhaps the author should write under the name "Martina James". A number of the marketing assistants nodded enthusiastically and wrote down the idea on their iPads.

"Try getting the book for no more than thirty thousand." Tweed proposed, after one of the editorial assistants argued how "genre strong" the novel was.

The next few submissions were given the thumbs down. The first one, a literary novel, "would fall between genres rather than straddle them." The second book to be dismissed was from an author whose last book flopped. "Bookscan figures don't lie. Her numbers just don't add up." Also, Margaret Duvall put a further nail into the coffin by remarking that "the author isn't marketable", meaning that she was too old and unattractive in her view. The third proposal was for a celebrity autobiography of a DJ from the nineteen seventies, who had also worked for the BBC. The first chapter touched upon his friendship with another celebrity who had been in the newspapers due to a sex scandal story.

"The last thing we need is to publish a possible paedophile," Tweed said.

"Think of the publicity though," Troy Jones replied. More than one person in the room shook their head, as though they were a vet who wanted to communicate that Jones was a dog who needed to be put down.

The next two books, a history of the battle of the Somme and a cold war thriller, were both met with enthusiasm. In regards to the latter John Burke mentioned how the agent now wanted the publishers to put in a pre-emptive offer of six figures.

"Call his bluff. He should know that he hasn't the clout to pull that kind of shit anymore. Just hint that you'll be hesitant about signing up other authors in his stable. That should give him a reality check and bring down the price," Martin Tweed remarked, smiling at the daring, or stupidity, of the literary agent in question. Or was it a triumphant grin that could be seen on his face? Publishers now had agents over a barrel, Sara had heard. Major players like Bradley House signed fewer books, for less money. Also, agents were not only kowtowing to the new austerity climate, instigated after the crash of 2008, but they were also still being stonewalled over low eBook royalties for their authors (of only 25% of net, as opposed to cover price, revenues). Agents could still command high advances for their marquee names, but their mid-list authors had seen their advances cut by more than half.

Much had been written during the past few months about how publishers and eBook platforms had colluded on setting high prices, but the untold scandal of the publishing industry was still that major publishers were underpaying authors on their eBook royalties; in a sense they were colluding on setting scandalously low royalty rates. The agents, fearful of upsetting the publishers lest they refused to sign new deals for their authors, remained silent over the issue despite their private frustration and ire. Joe Simpson was one of the few authors who had broken the omertà over the problem. Sara considered how agents were now representing the interests of the publishers, rather than their writers. Indeed it was said that many authors, who had signed old contracts before the emergence of Kindle, were on a royalty of 50% of net revenues. Publishers had never envisioned eBooks taking off, therefore they could afford to offer attractive royalties on sales that they believed would never exist. But eBooks now accounted for over half the market in certain genres. Publishers had threatened agents and told them to have their authors sign new amended contracts of 25% – otherwise they would refuse to release their backlist books in a digital format (and also refuse to give them back the rights to publish elsewhere).

Sara and Polly shared a look and a smile as a few pot shots duly began to be fired across the table while further proposals were discussed. John Burke mentioned how "the marketing would need to be done properly" for one novel. Max Souness said that, "As long as the publicity department thinks it can generate coverage for the book it should sell." Chaz Connelly hinted how the majority of submissions that Julian put forward were from authors represented by literary agents who played in his cricket team.

Just over half way through the meeting Eddie Woolly decided to have his monthly rant too: "Why are we solely publishing for the supermarkets? We should be commissioning good books and having faith that they will sell in bookshops. Rather than chasing the next Lee Child and Helen Fielding we should be looking to sign up the next Paul Auster and Henry Fielding... Amazon and Tesco are the devil, not a golden calf that we should all be worshipping at the feet of... We should act as if Amazon doesn't exist."

Sara often sympathised with Eddie when he went off on such rants. Sooner or later, if bookshops continued to close down, he would be out of a job that, sometimes, he seemed to enjoy. Yet in terms of his philosophy regarding publishing he was, at best, swapping deckchairs on the Titanic. The old world was gone. Waterstones, far more than the supermarkets, had been responsible for Waterstones demise. The likes of Bradley House were no longer all powerful Gods of profit and culture. Amazon and Tesco were not the devil. They were just big companies reacting to and taking advantage of the book market as best they could, just like Bradley House (albeit Bradley House hadn't been quite as successful over the past few years). What Eddie didn't realise, or refused to realise, was that people liked Kindle. Kindle was convenient, offered more choice and (aside from certain titles published by the major houses) was cheaper.

Apparently, Sara heard, it used to be that commissioning editors ultimately decided the books a publisher would publish – and the sales team were given the catalogue and instructed to go out and sell the list. More so now though the sales team decided which books would be signed-up. They often directed the editorial team to find titles that were riding a trend, or that the supermarkets were interested in (such as vampire fiction, Scandinavian crime or ghost-written autobiographies of C-list celebrities). It also used to be the case that publicists had more freedom and they could and would champion a book (instead of merely being told to work on the book that month that the publishers had paid the largest advance for). Rather than championing books nowadays though people often disowned them before they even went to print, fearing that they might be linked to a flop that could cost them their job. Debut authors were often too much of a risk. The safest bet was to just sign authors who were on TV. "We need to find the Jamie Oliver of History," someone had remarked at the meeting. "Why don't we commission an actor from EastEnders to front a crime novel and just get a ghost to write it?"

The old world was gone – and it was far from a brave new one, populated by goodly creatures. Publishers now looked to screw over agents. Agents looked to screw over publishers. Both publishers and agents looked to screw over authors. Supermarkets looked to screw over publishers, demanding greater discounts and stocking fewer titles. Everybody seemed to be screwing each other over, Sara thought – it was all lust and little love between them. Pleasing shareholders had become more important than pleasing readers, but what they should have realised was that by pleasing readers the publishers would eventually please shareholders. Despite all the above though Sara enjoyed her job and Bradley House still produced some good books (as well as its fair share of dreadful ones).

In regards to the last book discussed at the meeting Martin Tweed had already finalised the deal (for an advance that most in the room considered was three times what it should have been). Bradley House was proud to announce that it would be publishing the diaries of a former leading Labour politician, David Preston-Whyte. Sara later found out that Preston-Whyte's wife was best friends with Mrs Martin Tweed – they did yoga together.

Sara smiled when, after the meeting, she heard Charlotte Hurst remark, "If only Preston-Whyte can sex up his diaries as much as his dossiers."

7.

To make up for him being absent the night before – and due to a client cancelling an appointment – Simon arranged to take Sara out for lunch after the acquisitions meeting. He whisked her off in a cab and took her to a new bistro, Auberge, which had opened up on the river in Chiswick.

They sat out on the terrace, which overlooked a pea green Thames flecked with sunlight. Sara was wearing a pleated poker dot cotton dress that Rosie had bought her for her birthday. Simon wore a cream summer blazer from Brooks Bros and shirt which was almost as white as his gleaming teeth.

The sound of the breeze, teams of rowers out on the river, and the murmur of other diners on the terrace filled the silences between the couple. Sara had the sea bass on a bed of green salad. Simon ordered the pasta. They made small talk. He was forever thumbing away on his Blackberry though and Sara frequently looked out upon the twinkling river, distracted. She was thinking about him. Adam. What was he doing? Was he working, writing? What book was he reading? Or was he spending his day chasing barmaids and drowning his sorrows in a bottle of vodka?

"Penne for your thoughts?" Simon joked, holding up some of his pasta on his fork.

"Sorry, I'm just thinking about work. I must have seemed a thousand miles away," Sara replied, snapping out of her reverie.

"I'm going to be thousands of miles away myself over the coming week. I've been asked to go out to the New York office. Paul and Lisa will also be coming on the trip. Would you like to join us? You could go shopping."

Paul was Simon's colleague. Sara tolerated rather than liked him. He was always talking – or bragging – about how much money he earned. Whenever Sara met up with him Paul would always ask her to introduce him to her model friends. Lisa worked as a secretary to both of them. Sara had only met Lisa a couple of times but she seemed friendly and fun.

"I've got to stay here and look after this new author unfortunately," Sara said, glad that she had an excuse not to join them all.

"When I get back I think we should have a talk, about where we are and where we're going," Simon stated, growing serious – as though they were due to talk over a business transaction.

Sara had both desired and dreaded the conversation that Simon was asking her to pencil in her diary. What was he proposing? Proposing? Perhaps only when he finally asked the question would Sara know her answer.

"Okay," she replied, not quite knowing what else to say. Just before the pregnant pause between them became too unnerving however Sara's phone rang. It was Adam Cooper.

"Hi Sara, I hope I'm not disturbing you."

"No, it's fine," she replied, genuinely pleased to hear from him – and not just because the call had rescued her from an awkward moment. She tried not to look across the table at her peeved boyfriend as she spoke. It was okay for him to take work calls during their time together, but not her.

"I just wanted to let you know that a charity I'm a patron of has asked me to give a talk at an event they're hosting this coming Sunday evening. I'll send over the details in an email. If you could let the charity and myself know should you be able to fit it into the schedule though, as they need to finalise arrangements."

"Ok, thanks. I'll let you know as soon as I get back to the office. Where is the talk going to be by the way?"

"The Lake District."

When Sara hung up the phone she smiled at Simon, but thought of Adam.

*

"So he wants to have a, or rather *the*, talk?" Rosie said later that evening, as the two friends went through their day and a bottle of wine together. They had just finished having a light supper. Sara had made her (infamous) lasagne. They were now sitting in the living room. Bulging book cases lined most of the walls, as did some framed prints from the National Gallery of some of Sara's favourite paintings – landscapes by Turner and Constable and portraits of Coleridge, Jane Austen and Keats. The two women sat at opposite ends of a large, leather sofa. Outside the evening sky glowed with the embers of dusk.

"I guess so," Sara answered, her face expressing anxiety rather than excitement.

"I thought you wanted to discuss things with him and have this sort of conversation?"

"I know. Be careful what you wish for and all of that. A fortnight ago I was complaining how I didn't want us to stay in limbo land in regards to the future, but limbo land seems a pretty attractive prospect now to having a conversation which may decide the rest of my life. The thing is, I still don't know what I want," Sara said, holding out her glass again, knowing only that she wanted a re-fill.

"You should consider yourself lucky. I'm going through such a dry spell that I'm thinking of having you set me up with your friend Eddie. He'd be so grateful for a girlfriend, I suspect, that he'd treat me like a princess. And I'd be willing to kiss a frog for that kind of treatment," Rosie said, with as much sincerity as humour.

"If you want to kiss a toad I can always try and set you up with Julian Smythe. He'd prefer it if you kissed his arse though," Sara said, the pair of them laughing as much from the wine as from the joke.

"The question is do you want to give Simon the kiss off? Or can you hear the sound of wedding bells in your mind?"

"Unfortunately they sound more like the death knell of a funeral. He used to be so sweet when I first met him. He went out of his way to win me. Now he just does enough not to lose me, I sometimes think. Maybe we're just all but married in name already."

I need to talk to Simon, not Rosie, about all of this, she thought.

Sara thought about what Victoria Glass had said in her recent interview. But Simon and she were failing at being friends. Would, could, they still succeed as husband and wife?

Noticing how sad and uncomfortable her friend was becoming Rosie decided to change the subject, by first asking Sara if there was anything on TV she wanted to watch – and then mentioning that her new author's ex-wife had been on a programme earlier, talking about Kate Middleton's style. Sara, who was still yet to form a firm judgement as to what she thought of Victoria Glass, asked her best friend what she thought of the alluring socialite.

"Well on the plus side it seems that she does, along with Kate, do plenty of work for the charities she's linked to. In her favour too she's not Elizabeth Hurley or Tamara Ecclestone. Whether this is a plus or minus, she has a figure that even you'd die for – or kill for. From reading some of the stories in the newspapers – and seeing the countless number of photos of her – she owns more pairs of shoes than Imelda Marcus... On the whole though I just don't like it when people are more famous than they are talented... But now you tell me, what do you think of the former Mr Glass, your author? From the pictures I've seen of him I wouldn't mind dying – or killing – to get hold of his body."

Sara laughed, but then remained coy on the subject when it came to her answer.

"I've yet to spend any real time with him. I promise I'll send you his plus and minus points soon though."

Adam Cooper was like a book that she had only got through the first chapter of. But she wanted to read on.

8.

Citrus-fresh sunlight flooded Sara's bedroom in the morning and she found herself opening Adam's message before Simon's. The author it seems had either been working long into the night, or was a very early riser, given the time the email had been sent. Adam had completed the answers for the questions that various magazines and websites had sent her. The tone was largely informal in the interviews, as it seemed Adam knew quite a few of the journalists and editors involved. Perhaps, because of the personal loyalty involved, they had stuck to the brief in regards to asking questions about the author's career and new book, rather than his private life.

"Would you like me to bring you anything back from New York?" Simon had messaged. Sara here thought about the song, *'Spanish Boots of Spanish Leather'*, which Adam had mentioned in passing during their conversation in the pub. The song tells the story of a woman who travels to Spain. She asks her lover if he wants her to send him any gift, but the man just misses his sweetheart and wants her to come back. In the end she extends her travelling and he concedes the relationship has ended by asking her to send him boots of Spanish leather. Reality always gets in the way of love and happy endings. Sara replied to Simon to just enjoy himself while he was away.

He had answered, *"I will. x"* inserting a winking smiley face too.

Sara sighed, either in exasperation that her boyfriend was developing the habit of sending emoticons, or in relief. She welcomed the breathing space she would get in their relationship while Simon was in New York. She spent a few minutes extra choosing her outfit for the day, which she would also need to wear for the event in the evening. She picked out her scarlet and black colour block shift dress from Episode, which accentuated her figure. She also pulled out her favourite pair of black heels, which she put in a bag and could change into at the end of the day.

When Sara got into work she called the bookshop in Hampstead to make sure all was well in regards to the arrangements for the book talk that night. She also called a number of local papers about covering the talks Adam was giving outside of London. She finalised some articles and interviews with the likes of *Forces News* and *Soldier Magazine*. All were obliging, having dealt with the author before. Sara had called one military publication and got through to a young, female journalist who had almost cooed on hearing the author's name and said that, once Adam was free, she would love to take him to lunch. "I've interviewed him before, he's very friendly," the journalist had said, mentioning how Adam had once taken her out to dinner. Sara wondered how friendly Adam had been towards the journalist – feeling curious, disapproving and perhaps even a little jealous.

Sara also received a couple of calls around midday. They were from hacks from the tabloids, asking for an interview with the author about his former wife. Sara lowered her voice and politely refused the requests. More than to her boss Sara felt she still had to answer to her conscience.

Towards the end of the day however Sara was summoned into Margaret Duvall's office.

"Darling, would you be a dear? I've somehow broken my Twitter account again and also forgotten my password... Also, I need you to book me a table at *The Midas*... Make sure you seat me near the door, in case I need to dash out for a cigarette... I remember when I was last there, I ran into Nicola Redriff, the celebrity chef. Her ex-husband, that ghastly man, has just been arrested I understand, for tax evasion. For years I always thought that she'd be the one to be arrested, either for taking drugs or for stealing recipe ideas from friends... I heard that her latest book, *Tarting It Up*, has flopped. It looks like the publishers will be seeing many unhappy book returns... When I saw her in the restaurant she was wearing a dress that showed off her figure, unfortunately for her... Now remember to keep your phone to hand when you're away. You never know when I may need you..."

Sara did her best to tune the publicity director out but still her bitchiness stabbed through like a stiletto. The marketing department were lazy, sales staff had been lucky with a few titles which papered over cracks of failures and many of the editorial staff walked around like the living dead, powerless to sign the books they wanted and pining for a golden age. Indeed if Margaret Duvall hadn't had to leave early to attend an appointment about getting laser eye surgery done she would have had a pointed comment ready to say to Sara about everyone in the building.

*

Adam's first talk was at an independent bookshop in Hampstead. The shop regularly held events and had sold seventy tickets or so, which was good for a summer's evening in London. Sara was both nervous and looking forward to seeing her author again, as if she were about to go on a date. She got to the bookshop early and re-touched what little make-up she was wearing and changed into some heels. Sara also sent a message to Simon to say she hoped he'd had a good flight. Maybe his flight had been delayed and he was still in the air though, as he failed to reply.

Sara was in conversation with a bookseller when Adam arrived. Again he was dressed simply yet smartly in a jacket, shirt and jeans. He smiled at her across the room, turning his head and looking at her strangely – as if gazing at her for the first time. They both worked their way through the ever increasing throng of people. Sara didn't know whether to shake Adam's hand to greet him or give him the ubiquitous, often phoney, double peck on the cheek kiss which was as endemic to publishing as it was to Paris. She chose neither. Adam seemed temporarily distracted as he scanned around to see where he could get hold of a glass of wine. Thankfully a bookseller came to his rescue.

"Thank you," Adam said warmly as the young woman handed him the glass. She was pale, pencil thin and a little awkward looking. Part Goth, part Emo, part something else that she would grow out of. She was wearing a black and white T-shirt with the line "I'm not old I'm just out of date" emblazoned upon it.

"Are you a Dwight Yoakum fan?" Adam added, taking in the phrase, a quote from a country song (he seemed to have an encyclopaedic knowledge of books, music and films Sara thought, remembering their conversation in the pub). The bookseller smiled and nodded, looking bashful, happy and pretty all at the same moment. Someone had finally recognised where the phrase came from and they appreciated it – and her.

"Let's just hope that the bookshop has as good a taste in wine as you do music," the handsome author remarked, downing half the glass in just one mouthful.

Blushes added colour into the girl's pallid cheeks. She was unable to speak, but her smile communicated how much her evening had been made by the exchange with the bestselling writer.

"You've got a nice crowd it seems," Sara said, as she gazed around her – pleased by the numbers – as the shy bookseller scurried away. There was a professional part of her which wanted to bolster her author's ego and also communicate to him how the publishers were doing a good job promoting his book.

"A fair number of them are friends; the rest may be seeking a cure for their insomnia. I'll look to keep them awake, or send them to sleep with my talk, accordingly. Thank you for coming by the way. I don't want you thinking that I'm one of these authors, or divas, who need their hand holding all the time though."

"No, it's no trouble. I'm interested in hearing you speak," Sara replied, grinning at Adam's knowing comment (too many author did indeed behave like divas, especially the men).

"Should you be free after the talk would you like to join us for dinner? A few of my old army friends are coming along tonight and we'll be having a meal afterwards. I should warn you though that half of them will spend the evening telling you some well trodden war stories and the other half will look to chat you up and get your number."

"I've already got their number, so to speak. My uncle was is the army. I've sat down with many an officer at a dinner before. I'll get my own back by telling them some well trodden stories about being a book publicist."

"Playing hard to get may only make them try harder. It'll doubtless be the married ones who'll try hardest though."

Sara laughed.

Having a bit of time to kill Adam suggested that they take a turn around the bookshop. He was interested in the books she had read and ones she would recommend. They found their way to the classics section and were like teenagers talking about their favourite albums or movies as they discussed certain books and authors. Adam insisted on buying his publicist a book – a beautifully bound hardback copy of the *Lyrical Ballads*. In return Sara insisted on buying her author a copy of one of her favourite novels, *Home of the Gentry* by Ivan Turgenev.

"It's a tragic love story," Sara said.

"Which true love stories aren't tragic?" Adam sorrowfully replied – but then attempted to smile, not wishing to bring down the mood.

Shortly afterwards Adam gave his talk. He spoke about his time in the army and how it had informed the plot of his latest novel. *Hidden Agenda* was a thriller about a soldier and whistle-blower, who is killed for writing a report on how the British government were complicit in supporting the drug barons in Afghanistan (in exchange for them not supporting the Taliban). The report also damns a leading politician for turning a blind eye to the atrocities the poppy growers committed against girls who attended school in Afghanistan. The novel's hero, John Powell, investigates the murder of his friend however and exposes the politician. The politician, who now works for the UN, escapes to a non-extradition country – but Powell tracks him down and murders him through forcing dollar bills down his throat.

"The villain of the piece, Anthony Hay, quotes Stalin at the beginning of the book saying that seven grams of lead, i.e a bullet, can cure any problem. Unfortunately I fear that we may need a tonne of lead to cure all the problems within the MOD, DFID and Foreign Office... A friend of mine operated as a sniper out in Helmand province. A therapist asked him what he felt when he pulled the trigger and murdered a member of the Taliban. His reply was that the only thing he felt was, "The recoil of the rifle." And he meant it... I also heard a story about a briefing, which took place after the siege of the Iranian embassy in the early eighties. A soldier from the SAS team who helped liberate the hostages was asked why he had shot one of the terrorist thirty-two times. His reply was, "I ran out of bullets." Sometimes a soldier's sense of humour gets so dark that it's difficult to see..."

After speaking for thirty minutes or so Adam then took questions from the audience.

"How much of John Powell is there in you?"

"Powell is brave, incorruptible and successful with women... Suffice to say to say *Hidden Agenda* is a work of my imagination, rather than being autobiographical."

"What's next for John Powell?"

"That's a good question. I'm tempted to have Powell go up against a bunch of divorce lawyers, but I suspect that not even my hero could come out of that conflict unscathed – or solvent..."

Adam received a deserved round of applause at the end and he was soon swamped with people coming up to him with their books for him to sign. Sara noticed how much readers loved him and/or his books – and she sensed how much Adam was genuinely grateful for anyone who had read one of his novels. Seeing how inundated the staff were Sara chipped in and helped carry books, pour wine and clear things up. Meanwhile Adam chatted with people, signed books and posed for photographs.

Adam occasionally, covertly, glanced over at his publicist as she kindly helped out a bookseller and politely smiled as one of his old army mates tried to chat her up. He also noticed how his publicist went up to each of the staff members towards the end and gave them a small present as a thank you for helping make the event a success. Sara similarly often glanced towards her author to make sure he was fine, as he signed a book or made someone laugh. A couple of times their eyes met and, for a second or so, it seemed like it was only just the two of them in the busy bookshop.

*

Adam again asked Sara out to supper with his friends but she regretfully declined. Clapham was at the other end of town and she still had a few things to get through in regards to work.

"Besides, you'll have plenty of time to suffer my company over the coming days, during the tour," she explained.

Sara finally received a message from Simon as she walked from the station to her home. Simon told her about the restaurant he was currently in – how they would have turned heads if they had walked in together. He also mentioned how he had bought some lingerie for her whilst killing time at the airport.

I'm looking forward to watching you try everything on – nearly as much as I'm looking forward to you taking it off. Wink. xx

A crescent moon, like a lop-sided grin, beamed in the night sky, as Sara lay in bed. She kept the curtains and window open to let the room breathe in a cooling evening breeze. But it wasn't just the sticky heat keeping her awake. She tossed and turned, like a princess with a pea beneath her mattress, as she recalled the scene just at the end of the event when a woman, claiming to be a writer herself, gave Adam her card, batted her eyelids and asked him to call her. The novel she was working on was doubtless as trashy as the outfit she wore, Sara ungenerously thought. Adam had taken the card and said something back, which caused the woman to toss her head back and give out a throaty laugh. Was he being flirtatious, or just friendly? Where was he now – at a club, with his old friends from the army? Or was he in someone else's bed, like the barmaid's? Sara had met his type before, for most of her adult life. Yet something inside of her argued that he was nothing like the various types of men she had met before. How many male models or City boys had she dated who could quote Byron? How many of them could make her smile, laugh or engage her as much as him? The problem was that Adam seemed too good to be true – and the comments Sara had read by his ex-wife still nagged at her. Underneath all the melancholy, intelligence and decency was Adam just like so many other men – shallow?

Like Simon.

9.

Adam looked a little worse for wear the following morning when he met Sara at the train station. She was dressed for comfort, rather than high style, in some white pumps, navy blue pedal pushers and a cream blouse. Sara couldn't help but notice that her author was, perhaps tellingly, wearing the same clothes from the previous evening.

"Morning," Adam remarked, squinting from the shimmering blue sky. He carried a much travelled canvas bag over his shoulder.

"Hi. Dare I ask, how was last night?" Sara said breezily, raising her eyebrow as Adam yawned and winced from his throbbing head. Her question was less innocent and off the cuff than it seemed. She wanted to know.

"It was fun catching up with people, not that I remember too much of where we went and what happened after dinner," Adam replied – Sara was not sure whether it was in jest or in earnest.

Adam didn't venture any more information and Sara thought it wasn't her place to ask, although she briefly checked for any lipstick on his collar or any hint of perfume on his clothes as they boarded the train.

As soon as he sat down Adam ordered a coffee, which gave him a jolt due to its foul taste rather than the caffeine in it. Sara then switched on her iPad and went through the updated schedule. They were now heading for Birmingham, where Adam was due to give a signing in a bookshop and in the evening he would be giving a talk to a large crime and thriller writing group. The following day they would travel to Manchester for another afternoon bookshop signing and then an evening event. After that they would head for the Lake District – and then it would be back to London for some stock signings in key shops and a publication dinner at the Army & Navy Club. She also updated him on the various reviews which were due to be coming out over the next fortnight.

As with before Sara sensed that Adam was barely taking notice of his itinerary. He appeared distracted, as well as tired. He nodded occasionally and made the odd vague comment as he gazed wistfully, or wanly, out of the window. His phone rang a couple of times but he cut off the call before answering. When Sara finished speaking however Adam appeared to come back to the land of the living. He turned to his publicist and remarked, "You seem wonderfully proficient Sara. Thank you for all the work you're doing. It's appreciated. What are your career plans, if you don't mind me asking? Do you want to remain in publicity, or work in editorial?"

"I'd like try my hand in editorial someday, but I'm not sure if I'm quite ready to be a Julian yet."

Adam let out a burst of laughter.

"God willing you'll never be a Julian. What do you think of him?"

Sara took a breath. She was tempted to be indiscreet, or rather honest, about her colleague but merely replied, unconvincingly, "He's a good editor."

"I think we both know that he can barely be considered a good person, let alone a good editor. Julian's a snob, but he should first look down on himself rather than others. He's part of a class of people that lacks class, whose idea of doing good is to read *The Guardian*, condemn football hooliganism and buy free trade bananas... In regards to him being an editor I'm yet to be convinced he reads my books, or anyone else's. He's slow to reply to emails, if he replies at all... Every time I meet him I play a game. I mention either a classic novel or a recent release that's been a bestseller, to see whether he's read it or not. Although Julian doesn't know it, he's never won a round of the game... He's also forever name dropping or mentioning bestselling books that he turned down – as if he's proud of it! In the army we would have called him a 'Rupert' – or something worse... Unfortunately, the truth is that he's probably working to the best of his abilities... You shouldn't think that you're somehow not ready to work in editorial yet Sara. You're well read, both in terms of the classics and contemporary fiction. You're also aware of what sells – and equally crucially how to sell things... Trust me, you're worth a hundred Julian Smythes, Sara, for all sorts of reasons."

Adam's compliment made Sara glow as much as the midday sun. She had thought about applying for editorial assistant jobs before, but something (or more than one thing) had always stopped her doing so. She felt she lacked confidence, or the contacts, or hadn't attended the right university, or that she would just be viewed as the blonde publicist.

Just as Sara was about to say something Adam's phone rang again. He checked who was calling and switched it off. His expression sunk into a gloom again and he decided to switch himself off too.

"Sorry for that. You've doubtless got some work to catch up on before we get to Birmingham. I thought I might use this time to catch up on some sleep though, if that's okay?"

Having served as a sentry in the army, learning from necessity to get bouts of sleep whenever he could, Adam soon drifted off. Sara often looked up from her iPad to take in her author. Despite his red-rimmed eyes and stubble, or perhaps because of them, he looked endearing when he was sleeping, Sara fancied. He needed taking care off. Rosie might have eyed him up, learned of his background, and have called Adam "a bit of rough". But when he opened his mouth Rosie would have realised what a smooth talker he could be – and she would take the rough with the smooth. Sara couldn't help but gaze upon Adam with a certain fondness – and attraction – in her expression. Whilst she was doing so a train steward passed by and said, "Would your husband like a pillow?"

10.

As the train was pulling into Birmingham Sara received an email from her boss.

Yet to hear news of an exclusive interview with Cooper talking about his marriage to Victoria Glass – and plugging the book. TV and The Mail *are everything. Raise your game. M.*

During the journey Sara had updated Margaret Duvall on certain things, including the articles that had gone live about Adam and the news that both the *Evening Standard* and *Daily Telegraph* would be reviewing the book due to conversations she'd had with their literary editors. But rather than acknowledging her successes her boss had looked to put her down and pressure her into betraying her author. Adam.

Sara stood transfixed, out of sorts, on the platform as she read the message over again. Her sun-kissed complexion even seemed to pale a little. Sara wanted to scream – get out of herself, or be herself. She felt flustered, angry, unappreciated. There was a part of her that wanted to cry, not just because of the message – but because of everything. Because of months of being over-worked and under-appreciated. Because as a publicist she had to smile all the time and nod her head. Because everyone thought she had a thousand friends but really she was lonely. Because she could never find the time and will to write her own book. Because should she say yes to Simon her wedding day might also feel like her funeral. Yet some of those feelings melted away as Adam warmly clasped her on the shoulder and looked her in the eyes, smiling kindly.

"Are you okay Sara? Would you like a bottle of water?"

"It's fine. Maybe it's the heat. I just feel a bit nauseous. Do you mind if I sit for five minutes?"

Adam led her to a bench. Without a word said they sat down and Sara leaned into him as he wrapped an arm around her.

I'm supposed to be looking after him. Not him me. Pull yourself together Sara. Or raise your game, as the inept hag said. But let me just stay here, like this, for a bit longer.

The sunny weather sapped the strength of a few, but for the most part an air of vibrancy and purpose filled the streets of Birmingham (for once?) as people showed off their new summer wardrobes and enjoyed the fine weather and feel good factor. The signing was due to take place at lunchtime in a bookshop within the shopping centre. Rather than check into their hotel first they headed over to the signing straightaway. Things went well. There was a small queue made up of fans and a few of Adam's friends from his army days. The laughter and conversation emanating from the corner of the shop where the signing was taking place drew in a few passing customers too, more women than men, and they sold another fifty copies of the new novel (as well as signing another fifty for stock – "a signed book is a sold book").

Adam and Sara thanked the staff and bought them some wine and chocolates for their staff room before venturing off to check into their hotel, foregoing the sights and cultural attractions of Birmingham. During their walk through the city centre Sara noticed that Adam received another couple of calls on his phone, which he rang off rather than answered. Was it just a persistent journalist, angling for a quote about his ex-wife? Or were they calls from a woman, or women, who'd he met? Every time they called and he didn't answer Adam certainly looked vexed, or sad. It wasn't that he was ignoring all of his calls either, just some. Sara noted he still took a call from his literary agent and his sister.

The hotel was pleasant enough. Sara had booked two rooms in advance next to each other. They checked in and freshened up.

Just before having a late lunch together Adam gave an interview over the phone to a radio station dedicated to service personnel. The presenter was apparently respectful of Adam's wishes that he didn't want to talk about his private life, or he just rightly felt that it wasn't news and there were more important things to cover. One of the issues the former soldier was asked about was the problem of Afghanistan being the principle grower of opium in the world – and supplying the illegal drug trade.

"A radical solution, which I'm not altogether endorsing and I'm sure that there are more qualified people in the world to look into it, would be for the West to buy the opium crop from the Afghans and thus prevent drug cartels from doing so... Or we should subsidise the Afghans to farm food rather than opium, which in the long and short term may ease the amount of foreign aid given to the country... The cost of paying the farmers an inflated price for changing what they grow would doubtless cost the West less than the money they currently burn in trying to tackle the problem of drugs from the other end. Governments and companies already buy ten percent of the world's opium for scientific and medical purposes, principally for the production of morphine..."

During Adam's interview Sara received a message from Simon.

Hi babe. Sorry if I've been off the radar. Am just heading to a breakfast meeting. I've got to seal the deal. Will be thinking of you though. Wink. xx

They decided to remain at the hotel for lunch. Neither of them knew of a nice restaurant in the city centre and both of them had work to catch up on before they had to leave for the event in the evening. Adam's agent had asked him to finish off his book proposal for his next deal and Sara had various emails to reply to.

Sara had a small glass of white wine over lunch, while Adam worked his way through the rest of the bottle. They chatted about all sorts, over several games of Scrabble (which Sara had downloaded on her iPad). She was nigh on addicted to the game and in Adam she seemed to have met her match. They spoke about their favourite works of Tolstoy – and favourite Pixar movies. They also discovered that they had both attended Catholic schools and chatted about their similar and different experiences. Sara also mentioned how much she was looking forward to visiting the Lake District. She could work it into their schedule to visit Dove Cottage and the Wordsworth

Museum. Adam said he'd be interested in seeing the cottage too.

Finally, I'm going, Sara thought to herself.

"The book tour will have a happy ending," Sara said, tapping the details of their sightseeing trip into her iPad.

Unlike too many other authors to mention, Adam took an interest in his publicist – rather than just talked about himself. He asked her about her career in modelling and why she had left the fashion world to join the publishing industry.

"There wasn't one reason... The catwalk began to stretch out before me and I felt like I was walking a mile each time I stepped out onto the runway... There are few women I've found, who are as unnaturally thin as you need to be as a model, who are also healthy and happy... I was tired of being called 'angel', 'honey' and 'sweetheart'. I wanted to be Sara... I also wanted to attend university and challenge myself in a different way... I love reading and ultimately I'd like to write a novel one day... I've already written a few short stories and a novella, which I've posted on the website Authonomy... I'm not expecting anything to come of it, but I enjoyed writing the stories and it meant something to me..."

Why am I telling him all of this? Why should he care?

"I was wrong earlier Sara. You're worth a thousand Julian Smythes."

Please don't let this be an act. Please let him be genuinely lovely. I want to believe that there is one smart, funny, decent guy out there – even if I can't have him.

11.

Sara finally turned off the iPad, breathed out and lay upon her back on the bed; keeping still so as not to muss up her hair or crease her dress. She told herself to use the window of time to call Simon, out of a sense of habit rather than from a real desire to do so. But she also told herself that he would probably be busy and it would be better not to disturb him. Things would change between them when he got back. But Sara didn't quite know how, or if the change would be for the better or for the worse. When she was younger she had realised that most relationships end badly, but in truth even when people were at their best things could still be a messy. "The job is never finished of painting the bridge to save it from rust," her father had once said, when he gave his daughter some relationship advice.

For just fifteen minutes she didn't want to think about work or her relationship with Simon. All she wanted to hear was the birdsong from out of her window. For just fifteen minutes she wanted some quietude to empty her cluttered head and think about nothing, or him. Sara still felt the strong and tender sensation from when he had held her briefly at the train station. She remembered some of the things he had said during the day. She pictured the scene again, when he had quoted Byron. He made her laugh – and her heart beat faster. Adam could tell a joke or give a compliment – or carry out a small act of kindness or generosity – and make someone's day.

Is he in his room now thinking about me? Now you're just being silly, acting like a teenager... Maybe he's just interested in barmaids and literary groupies... The last thing he probably wants right now is a meaningful relationship, after coming out of his marriage. But the last thing I need right now is a meaningless fling... Life doesn't mirror plots from Jane Austen novels... You're not a character in some romantic comedy... Maybe he's conscious of not making any advances because we need to have a professional relationship... Remember how he treated his ex-wife. He drinks, she was right about that. Why would she have not been honest about his womanising too? He'll hurt you in the end, if anything happens. That's what men do... But nothing can or will happen between us. I'm with Simon – and I don't want to hurt him...

It was 5.30. Sara had arranged to meet Adam in the hotel bar at 5.45. From there they would get a taxi to the university, where the Birmingham Crime & Thriller Writers' Association had booked out a lecture theatre to host a talk by Adam. She checked herself in the mirror one last time, straightened her already straight fringe and decided to go downstairs a little early.

Adam was already at the bar when she got there. Music was playing in the background, Lionel Richie's 'Stuck on You'. Adam was cradling a whisky and looking down into the tumbler, expecting to find the solution to something there perhaps. He'd shaved and was wearing a shirt, jacket and trousers. "Adam may be a squaddie at heart, but he was comfortable at being an officer too," one of his army buddies had remarked to her at the event in Hampstead. He scrubbed up well.

Rosie would definitely take the rough with the smooth. And so would I.

Her perfume filled his nostrils as she came up behind him and Adam came back to life, stood up and put his drink down. He turned towards Sara. His eyes widened in astonishment and pleasure as he took in his publicist – and her dress. She was wearing her Jacques Vert black and white shift dress, inlaid with lace work. Rosie joked that she should only wear it sparingly – and inside – for fear of causing traffic accidents. It was pretty, elegant and she always felt in bloom when she wore it. Sara told herself that she packed the dress because it was suitable as summer and evening wear – but really she picked it out because she thought that Adam might like it. Which he did – and then some. Her eyes shone as brightly as the L.K. Bennett polished black heels she wore, when she took in his reaction. Her lips were fuller ("kissable" – Adam would later think to himself) from the soft red lipstick she wore. A pair of silver oval drop earrings sparkled beneath her blonde hair every time Sara turned her head. She also wore the small silver cross that her mother had bought for her for Christmas a couple of years ago (Simon never liked her wearing it).

It's not that she looks beautiful. It's that she is beautiful – kind, funny and smart. Indeed her attractiveness sometimes works against her, blinding people to the other good things about her... She's turning more than just my head in the bar, but I'm seeing so much more than they are.

Adam liked her, more than he wanted to admit to himself – let alone to Sara. He was worried however that she was just a distraction, from the hurt he still felt from his divorce. And how much love did he have left in his heart for anyone after what he had recently been through? His glass wasn't even half full; there was just half an ice cube left at the bottom of the tumbler, figuratively and metaphorically. He felt more like a widower than divorcee sometimes. Victoria had been everything to him, but was now nothing to him. Adam also didn't want to ruin a friendship, or their professional relationship, by saying something to Sara he would regret.

I don't want to hurt her. And don't hurt yourself again Cooper. If you fall no one will catch you. Life doesn't play itself out like a love song. But she's got a way about her...

12.

They got to the venue early, as Sara had arranged for Adam to be interviewed by the local paper. After the interview they met Frank Porter, the social secretary for the writing group. He was a retired RAF officer and a published author, although, for the past ten years, he had yet to secure a deal with a major, or minor, publisher. He was seventy and looked more like David Niven than David Beckham. Margaret Duvall wouldn't have called him "marketable". Yet he was a kindly soul and good writer. Before the event Adam also found himself talking to Justin Courtney, a young black man. Justin wrote historical crime, set during the Great War. He had secured a meeting with a top agent a year ago through the strength of his manuscript. When they met however the agent advised Justin to write something more gritty or urban, or write a Zadie Smith-like novel about an immigrant living in the inner city. When Justin explained that he had lived in Britain all his life – and grew up in the suburbs – the agent seemed disappointed. Adam, impressed by the concept and strength of the central character in Justin's idea, said that he would take a look at the book and put him in touch with his own agent.

The audience numbered close to a hundred. Adam first spoke about his books, their formula and how he went about writing and researching his thrillers. The main portion of the evening though was dedicated to the writing group asking the author questions. Understandably the would-be writers in the audience asked about the best way to obtain an agent and publishing deal. Similarly, the people who were already published or self-published asked about tips in regards to author promotion and publicity. At which point, to her surprise, Adam invited Sara to join him on the stage. He encouraged her to give her view, both on publishing in general and publicity. She didn't balk from a sense of realism and articulated how publishers were publishing fewer books and consequently agents were developing fewer new authors. But there was now another way, which her employers may have deemed heresy should they have heard her recommend it. Authors could contact independent publishers themselves (although she warned the group not to pay a vanity publisher to produce and market their work). But the major publishers and literary agents were no longer the gatekeepers. An author now also possessed the option of setting up their own publishers on Kindle and other digital platforms. In terms of the genres of crime and thrillers Kindle sales alone could provide an income for talented, prolific writers. Should an author want physical copies of their books available there was Createspace and lulu.com. Sara also provided some tips for the audience on promoting books through Twitter, Goodreads, contacting book bloggers and other hubs for spreading the word. She grew in confidence as she spoke and, like Adam, gave sound editorial advice. Sara even agreed to read a couple of manuscripts and give some feedback via email for a few people.

"I'd be happy to look at the opening chapters of your novel. It'll be good practice. A friend of mine has recently encouraged me to consider a career in editorial... There's a book in everyone, but it's often the case that that's where it should stay... Most debut books are over written, or not sufficiently re-written... Be wary of digital book promoters however, who promise the world but in the end just deliver a number of fake followers on twitter..."

Adam and Sara laughed and joked on the stage, as well as providing advice (which proved both encouraging and dispiriting – depending on the attitude of the recipient). They shared looks which they thought were private, but everyone in the audience could see that there was a spark between them. Old-fashioned chemistry. A shared sense of humour and a shared attraction.

Towards the end of the event, while Adam signed books for members of the audience, the social secretary approached Sara and asked if she would be willing to come back and give a talk by herself for the group next year. She was equally surprised as she was pleased by the invitation – and said yes.

"Thank you. Mr Cooper will be welcome to come back too of course. You make a great couple, or double-act, so to speak."

*

After the event Sara and Adam chose to walk back to the hotel, rather than call a taxi. There was a refreshing, cooling breeze riding in the balmy air and a ripe moon showcased a sky studded with stars. They both walked slowly and followed as scenic a path as possible, as if neither of them wanted the night to end. When they reached the hotel they ordered a drink and sat outside on a bench in the garden. They chatted about each of their families. Sara mentioned her sister, who regrettably she rarely saw nowadays. During their teens her sister, Carly, resented Sara for the attention she received from boys and their parents for being a model. She had envied her success.

"Ironically I envied Carly for her anonymity. For growing up in a normal environment, with real friends, doing what she wanted... We don't actively argue. Partly because we just don't see each other, which is a shame as she's due to have a baby later in the year and I'd like to be a better aunt than I was – am – a sister..."

In was only in telling Adam how she felt that she fully realised it. Sara made a promise to him, as well as to herself, that she would get in touch with her sister when she got back to London.

The author – who preferred to write about his issues rather than talk to people about them – also opened up. Although he had only known Sara for a week he felt a strange, but strong, sense of trust and admiration towards her.

"I wanted to live near my parents, partly to keep an eye on them as they're becoming a bit frail. I must be the only person to have moved from Richmond to Eltham this year... My parents did a good job bringing me up, as much as I brought myself up when I hit my teens... I grew estranged from my parents, as well as my brother and sister, in my early twenties. I couldn't really talk to them about my time in Afghanistan... The more I isolated myself the more they would try to reach out to me... Work, writing, saved me when I came back from Helmand though... Strangely, when they stopped trying to work me out, they accepted me more... I often visit my parents and regularly go for a drink or meal with my brother and sister... I'll introduce you to them all at the dinner next week. My sister in particular would love to meet you. My parents would enjoy meeting you too. You're a good Catholic girl – with a devilish sense of humour... You should come around for lunch or dinner one Sunday, if you want."

I want.

Adam realised that he was speaking to Sara more as a friend, or even girlfriend, than publicist. *But it feels right. Let her in.*

*

Would I let him in if he knocked on the door?

Sara knew the answer to her question before she even asked it, as guilty as she felt when she saw the missed call from Simon. His voicemail said that he was now out for the evening.

Speak tomorrow, babe. Wink.

Sara was back in her hotel room, lying on the bed. Her dress was hanging up on the wardrobe door, opposite her. She smiled and almost laughed as she pictured the look on Adam's face in the bar earlier, when he had turned with his eyes lit up on seeing her in the dress. Rosie might have called Adam ruggedly handsome, but Sara was attracted to his good nature and his sense of humour, which shone in his boyish/roguish expression. As Sara lay in bed, half reading a novel, she also listened to various songs on her iPad (by Elton John, Michael Bublé and – of course – Billy Joel among others). Maybe the wine fuelled her imagination, but it seemed that all the love songs made sense and resonated, as if composed for her and how she was feeling. She had seldom, if ever, thought of Simon like she thought of Adam when listening to certain lines from her favourite songs. Something sang in her heart. But maybe it was just all down to the wine, she mused.

Behind her hotel room door Adam raised his hand, to knock. *Will she let me in?* His heart was galloping, like a wagon train of horses out of control. *I can't stop thinking about her. And it's not just the wine.*

Yet Adam paused, and lowered his hand, reining in his heart. *Life doesn't play itself out like a love song.* If it had been any other woman he would have knocked on her door.

Don't hurt her.

13.

Grey clouds smudged the sky. Rain slapped upon the window in the morning and woke Sara up before her alarm. An annoying draught also whistled through a thin gap between the pane and frame. The birdsong from yesterday had disappeared too.

Sara reached over to the bedside table and checked her phone for any messages from Simon, but it only flashed with a number of emails from work. Although Simon had not made the greatest of efforts to get in touch since being in New York Sara still felt guilty in having ignored him over the past day or so. She also felt guilty in relation to the thoughts and feelings she'd experienced for Adam. Although a few boyfriends had cheated on her over the years, Sara had never been unfaithful. In some ways yesterday felt like a dream. Let it remain a dream, a fancy, Sara told herself.

When she met Adam downstairs at breakfast she reverted to a more formal stance towards him. She wasn't rude or cold, but Sara did act in a far more pronounced business-like manner – similar to when they had first met. She talked about the weather and the forthcoming signings and events. Any other conversation seemed stilted. Sara was also conscious of mentioning, on more than one occasion (during breakfast and their train journey to Manchester) that she had a boyfriend. Adam duly took the hint and, although he still tried to crack the odd joke and have Sara open up to him, he too, for her sake, behaved like an author should with his publicist. He took consolation from the fact that at least he hadn't succumbed to temptation and knocked on her hotel door the night before.

Life plays itself out through sad songs.

For the most part during the train journey they both sat in silence and worked. Adam finally finished his book proposal and emailed it off to his agent. To ease the tension and protracted silences Adam also pretended to be asleep on the train. It was while he pretended to do so that Sara locked herself in the toilet and cried, for reasons that she couldn't quite understand. The heart has its own reasons.

*

The signing at the bookshop in Manchester was not quite a complete wash-out, but they only sold around a quarter of the books that they had sold in Birmingham. The events manager at the shop and Sara made certain excuses – blaming the rain or that people had started to go away for their summer holidays – but Adam had taken part in enough events to know that not everything works and he was neither angry nor upset. He filled up some of the time by speaking to a few creative writing students from the nearby university, who had come to meet him. As well as providing some advice and encouragement Adam also kindly bought the students a book each – signing and dedicating the copies.

Towards the end of the event a pudding-faced journalist turned up from the local paper to profile the author. He first asked Adam questions about the book and the current state of affairs in Afghanistan (the journalist having not read the former and being ill-informed about the latter). He then asked Adam if he would like to comment about the rumour that his ex-wife was dating James Cardinal, the wild-boy Shakespearean actor.

"No comment," the ex-soldier replied, with more than just a little steel in his voice and expression.

The warning shot across his bow was sufficient enough to encourage the hack to stick to his brief of just talking about the book. After the journalist left Sara apologised to her author, saying that she had spoken to him beforehand about the parameters of the interview.

"There's no need to apologise Sara. I know it wasn't your fault. He's a journalist. If a vulture spots a carcass he's going to want to feast," Adam remarked philosophically.

*

The rain continued to fall. After the signing Adam suggested that they have lunch. He recommended a nice, independent Italian restaurant which was a short walk away (remembering how Sara had mentioned the previous evening that Italian was her favourite food). But she said that she had to get to the hotel and catch up on some work. She felt guilty in snubbing him – and lying to him – but Sara felt guiltier still in regards to Simon. This had been the longest period, for some time, that they hadn't spoken to each other. She needed to go back to the hotel and call him.

As Sara got back to her room she received another email from Margaret Duvall. The first part mentioned how she had locked herself out from her twitter account again and the second part asked for an update on whether any of the newspapers had bitten in regards to an interview with Adam Cooper. Sara was more than tempted to open up the mini bar after reading the message, but she merely sighed and poured herself a glass of water.

In contrast to the hotel in Birmingham, where her room had looked out upon a garden and some pear trees at the back of the hotel, Sara now gazed upon a half empty staff carpark and some over-filled bins. She felt compensated however as she noticed a card by the phone in her room, advertising that the hotel offered its guest thirty minutes of complimentary international calls. As phoning Simon on his mobile would be costly she decided to take advantages of the offer. It would now be morning in New York and she hoped to catch him before he left for work. She would doubtless spend more time listening to him, rather than talking, when they shared their week but that was fine. After all, her week had so far involved possibly falling for another man.

"Hello, Simon Keegan's phone," a woman answered, professional politeness mixed with slight confusion from the strange number coming up on the caller register.

"Come back to bed babe. You've played secretary enough on this trip. You need to role play something else," Simon announced suggestively in the background.

"Hello, who is this?" the woman, which Sara now recognised as being Lisa, Simon's secretary, asked.

"Simon's ex-girlfriend."

Lisa gasped, but before she could say anything else Sara hung up the call. Sara bent over, as if she were about to be sick, and then fell onto the bed. Blood rushed up to her face – she was embarrassed and ashamed. And then her face grew redder with anger... She felt dizzy and sobbed, almost to the point of choking – gasping for air. Sara replayed Lisa's voice – and his – over in her head again and wanted the ground to swallow her up. Or she wished that the ground could swallow them up. Bury all trace of him.

She received a call back from him, but ignored it, throwing the phone down on the bed as if it were poisonous. His snake-like face popped-up on the screen and she winced. The hurt almost manifested itself into a physical pain. The room seemed to spin and Sara curled up in a ball and clutched a pillow, as if to anchor her down.

I hate him.

Again her phone flashed up with a call from Simon – and she ignored it. If he wanted to talk to someone he could talk to *her*, his *fun and friendly* secretary.

Sara finally reached over and took a sip of water. Her hand trembled as she did so.

He's dead to me.

It was the one sin she couldn't forgive. It was over, she determined. She felt like the past six months had been a waste, or a lie at the best. She wouldn't fight for him. *She* could have him – and he would cheat on her accordingly.

Tears streamed down her cheeks as Sara gently rocked upon the bed, clutching the pillow again – feeling dead to herself.

All men are bastards.

14.

Tired, physically and emotionally, Sara eventually drifted off to sleep. When she woke her eyes were still puffy and she felt like someone had a cut a piece out of her. She mechanically replied to a few emails on her iPad but then picked up her phone, which seemed to now weigh as heavy as a brick in her hands. She listened to the voice messages from Simon.

The first thing Sara noticed was that he seemed to be whispering – and the acoustics were strange. She realised that he must have retreated into the hotel bathroom and was talking quietly, to avoid Lisa from hearing him. The first message desperately – and unconvincingly – urged Sara not to get the wrong idea. He knew that Sara was on the other end of the line when Lisa picked up the phone and he was just playing a joke on her. He begged her to call him back immediately. During the second call, which followed shortly afterwards, Simon apologised. They had both got drunk the night before, celebrating a deal. "She means nothing to me." Again he asked her to call him. "We need to talk. You shouldn't throw the past six months away over just one night. This could make us stronger." He argued that if she should had have cheated on him then he would have forgiven her. "What we have is too good... We need to be grown-ups about this..."

Sara didn't call Simon back. She did call Adam however and said that she would be unable to make the event this evening, a dinner and book signing organised by one of his fellow officers from his old regiment. Adam said he was disappointed that she couldn't make it, but he would be fine flying solo. The main thing was for her to feel better. He asked if he could get anything for her from the pharmacist, but she said that it would hopefully just be a twenty-four hour thing. She just needed some rest – and to be left on her own.

Adam had been sweet and understanding on the phone, but the last person she wanted to spend the evening with was another serial cheat, or "love rat", as Rosie often termed it when she wrote an article for her local paper. How different was he really from Simon? Sara didn't feel like putting on an outfit and make-up and smiling in the face of the world at the event tonight, which would be filled with (happy) couples having dinner together or soldiers trying to chat her up.

Shortly afterwards Sara called Rosie and spent an hour or so talking – and crying – on the phone to her friend. Rosie tried – and to a small extent succeeded – to console her flatmate. Simon didn't deserve her, Rosie posited. Sara was right to want to end things. It was better to find out now what he was like, rather than later. She couldn't commit to him because deep down Sara knew he was more of a Wickham than Darcy – and that she didn't love him. She was happy to collect any things belonging to Sara that Simon still had at his apartment. After talking to Rosie Sara switched on the TV and removed more than just a bottle of water from the mini-bar.

*

It was late by the time Adam got back to the hotel from the dinner. The event had gone well. He had caught up with various old friends from the regiment and he'd sold over a hundred books (crucially Sara had arranged for an independent bookshop, registered with Bookscan, to sell copies of the novel so that any sales would help in breaking the book into the bestseller lists). Yet there was a hole in the evening, for Sara not being there. Adam had been tempted to apologise on the phone earlier, should he have somehow done something wrong to upset her. She had behaved in a distant way towards him all day.

Instead of his publicist Adam found himself sitting next to a foreign correspondent, Tara Deaver, over dinner. They had first met – and slept together – during his time in Afghanistan. She was smart, sexy and they had been under fire, as well as under the sheets, with each other. Tara was looking good. She had bought a Karen Millen black faux-leather panelled dress to celebrate her recent promotion. Her dress was revealing – and she little disguised her desire to spend the night with Adam.

"She's on a plate for you mate, as your last course tonight," the organiser of the dinner had whispered to Adam during dessert.

For all of Tara Deaver's charms though Adam spent most of the evening thinking about someone else. It wasn't due to Adam still feeling raw from his divorce that he politely declined the journalist's invitation to come back to her hotel for a drink. No. If he would have spent the night with Tara Adam would have strangely felt that he was being unfaithful to Sara.

But how can you fight for someone when they don't want to be won? If she's happy in her relationship I should just disappear.

Adam received a text message. Tara asked if he was still awake. She was still buzzing – and had some coke to give them an even bigger buzz. She could be with him in ten minutes. He turned off his phone. A year ago, or a day before he had met Victoria, he would have called her back. Sex and drink were great tonics. But Adam wanted something different from life, love, now. Not a Tara. Or a Victoria even. They were game players, as he had once been. He wanted...

Sara.

The only game she would want to play with me was Scrabble, he smilingly thought.

*

Sara was a lot more self-conscious standing in the hallway, about to knock upon a hotel door, than Adam had been the night before. Partly because, it must be said, Adam had had more experience in knocking on the hotel doors of the opposite sex over the years.

She had initially struggled with the decision. She told herself that she wanted revenge on Simon. She also told herself that she would be using Adam, as Adam had probably used other women before. She had been unable to sleep and so had been listening for her author to return whilst reading one of his old novels. During a love scene in the book Sara thought of Adam Cooper rather than his hero John Powell.

She had kept her phone on silent, but noticed that Simon had called repeatedly. Already she was becoming bored and annoyed, rather than angry, in regards to her ex-boyfriend. She was also beginning to feel content and grateful that she was free of him. Free to do what she wanted. Rosie had rightly reminded Sara how she had said, on more than one occasion, that she felt trapped in the relationship. "You've had a lucky escape," her flatmate had argued. Sara decided she would return her sapphire earrings.

He can re-gift them to his secretary... Heaven can send him another Domestic Goddess.

Her heart beat faster as she heard a number of revellers along the corridor getting out of the elevator. She was wearing her pearl-coloured silk pyjamas. She had thought about wearing her normal clothes, or putting on an evening dress. Should she have been in a movie or a Danielle Steele novel she would have been wearing a robe with lingerie underneath it, she mused. But she was neither in a film nor a novel.

What would happen after he opened the door? Where would this leave them personally and professionally? What if he rejected her? But as Sara moved her hand forward to knock on the door she tried to ignore her doubts. Several drinks from the mini bar helped dilute them too. The future could, or couldn't, take care of itself.

But this is wrong. This isn't you... If ever I spend the night with him, I want him to make love to me. Not me pretending to be a Lisa.

Rather than knock upon the door Sara merely gently pressed her palm against it, imagining the door was his chest and she could feel his heartbeat – in tune with hers. Melancholy, more than ardour, shaped her features.

15.

Amber sunlight poured through the curtains of Sara's room the following morning. She woke to the sound of bin men rather than birdsong. Her head throbbed a little and she drank half a bottle of water to rehydrate herself. She stood before the mirror, her bob far from Louise Brooks-like and her eyes half-closed.

You've looked and felt better... At least he might now believe I was too ill to attend the event last night, on seeing me like this.

She wanted to go home, to cocoon herself from the imminent fall-out of ending things with Simon. How honest should she be with various people explaining why it was all over? He should feel ashamed of his actions, but she would be the one embarrassed when telling people about it. It felt like it would sting each time she would have to say that he cheated on her. She wanted her own bed. Rosie would take care of her too.

Yes. It was best all round it she went back to London. Even though nothing had happened last night, Sara would still feel uncomfortable around Adam. Sara could deny it to him, but she couldn't deny it to herself that she had feelings for a man who she hadn't even known for a week.

*

Grey clouds ambled across the sky. The sun still tried to lighten the scene although, by the time Sara stood with Adam outside the hotel waiting for her cab to take her to the train station, it seemed like it was fighting a losing battle.

Adam proved understanding when Sara let him know about her desire to return to London. He was concerned rather than angry or upset. She seemed genuinely ill and he sensed that there was something else wrong too. Sara said she would send an email whilst on the train in regards to any info he might need for the event that night in Cumbria. She also gave him his train ticket back to London.

"It's a shame that you're going to miss out on a trip to the Lake District. I guess this was not the happy ending to the tour that you'd envisaged," Adam remarked, breaking the silence between them. On the surface the scene was merely that of an author saying goodbye to his publicist and thanking her for the work she had done over the past week or so. But it was unspoken that more was being said. If the eyes were the mirror to the soul they shared a couple of soulful looks.

"We've both read enough Turgenev to know that there are no happy endings," Sara replied, as much to herself as to Adam. It was her time to stare distractedly – and sadly – into the distance.

"It would be nice to see you again Sara."

"You'll see me again at the publication dinner, don't worry."

That's not what I meant.

Oh God. That's not what he meant.

"And I may get to work on your paperback and next hardback, if you want to give me a second chance after abandoning you like this." She said it as a joke, but Sara again suffered a twinge of guilt for leaving Adam to his own devices.

"Sara, you're a lovely person. I'd give you a second, third and fourth chance – and twice on a Sunday – if need be. It's more important to know though that you can give yourself a second chance. You should apply for a position in editorial if that's what you want – and also write your novel. Have faith in yourself. I read something recently, saying that there's never been a summer that wasn't followed by winter – but there's never yet been a winter that wasn't followed by spring."

There was a pause, pregnant with recognition and surprise, as Sara realised that Adam had quoted from the story that she had posted up on Authonomy. Light and loveliness shone again in her expression. Simon had never read her story (although he did lie once and say he'd started reading it). Even Rosie had only glanced at her novella in a cursory way. Her smile made him smile.

"You took the time to read my novella? Why?" she asked, disbelief mingling with gratitude.

"Why? Because you're worth it," he replied, humour mingling with sincerity. *Because you said that it meant something to you. And you've started to mean something to me.*

Her heart skipped a beat and then thrummed faster.

"You know, I sometimes think that you're too good to be true," she finally remarked, reflectively.

"I'd prefer to be less good – and truer – if it meant that you would give me a second chance Sara."

They moved closer towards each other on the stone steps of the hotel; his eyes, brimming with affection and something else, were fixed upon her.

They'd found their moment.

A brace of smokers and other guests and members of staff streamed between them however as it started to rain and they rushed up the steps to take shelter in the hotel lobby. At the same time a receptionist came out to inform Sara that her taxi had arrived. The rain fell more heavily. The sound drowned out something that Adam whispered to her. A pot-bellied cab driver, with a cigarette hanging out of his mouth and a shirt half hanging out of his trousers, abruptly picked up Sara's suitcase and headed towards his car, grunting something in Mancunian as he did so.

They'd lost their moment.

Sara hurriedly said goodbye. Adam said something in reply, but again she couldn't decipher it over the loud shush of the shower. The cab driver grunted again. She rushed down the steps and headed towards the car, the rain running down her cheeks like tears. The car pulled away – to the sound of the driver cursing that his cigarette had been extinguished by the rain. Sara craned her neck and turned to see if Adam was still there. If she saw him look back he would know that she cared, like in the movies. But he'd already disappeared back into the hotel.

I should've told him how I felt.

I should've kissed her.

There are no happy endings...

16.

The train journey back to London was long – and felt longer. Sara tried to read, but couldn't concentrate. Scrabble was less than half the fun without him too. Sara was surer about her decision to leave Simon than she was in not staying with Adam and seeing the tour through. She sent an email to Adam about the event – and also any other pertinent information to do with the publicity campaign. She forwarded on the news that *The Mail on Sunday* and *CrimeTime* would be reviewing the book.

Sara finally received a reply to her email later that evening, when she was at home. She was still awake, watching a film with Rosie. Unfortunately even half a bottle of wine – and half a Toblerone – did little to lift her spirits. She hoped that the message from Adam would. But it didn't. Adam merely thanked her for her email and mentioned that the charity dinner had gone well and plenty of books had been sold. There was nothing said about how they had left things outside the hotel. There was nothing indicating that he wanted to see her again, after the launch party.

We missed our moment. I missed my moment.

Sara consoled herself with the thought that she wasn't ready for another relationship anyway.

That evening she wrote to Simon. She explained that she wanted to end things. It was for the best. There had been something missing from their relationship for some time. Maybe it had never been there in the first place. She didn't want him to contact her for a week or so. She wanted to be left alone. Rosie would be in touch with him shortly, to arrange to collect her belongings from his apartment.

Within fifteen minutes Simon emailed Sara back, begging her to forgive him. He knew he'd done wrong, but this was the only time that he'd been unfaithful. He wanted to build bridges. Sara replied, reiterating that it was over – and asked him not to contact her for a week. Within ten minutes he emailed back – and burnt bridges. She was being unfair, he argued (ranted) – and she called herself a Christian? He was glad it was over too. She bored him, in and out of bed. Simon took an unpleasant pleasure in confessing to Sara that he had cheated on her numerous times, with numerous women. He would find someone else, someone better, easily – given his prospects. His tone was often similar to a spoilt child having a tantrum. Sara turned off her phone and shook her head in disappointment and pity. But she also felt free, content that she could write another chapter into her life.

17.

Sara returned to work. For once the office floor was a hive of activity, as they were expecting the TV comedian Duncan Ferris to come to the building and sign a new book deal (the ghost writer had already finished the first two chapters). Ferris was famous for swearing on programmes before the watershed and making jokes about the Women's Institute. The comedian's oleaginous business manager made sure he accompanied his client, to reiterate how he wanted the publishers to pay the advance into their off-shore company account. The agent explained how his "socially divisive" client didn't like paying tax to "the Tory government," although it remained unspoken how Ferris had also avoided paying tax under the previous administration too.

After the cooing, tweeting and clapping was over Sara was immediately called into Margaret Duvall's office (after her boss had finished smoking a cigarette on the roof). Margaret played the school mistress and matriarch and informed Sara that she was disappointed in her for not securing a big interview piece with her author.

"You've let me down... And you've let the team down."

Sara let the words wash over her. The main thing was she hadn't let herself or Adam down.

Margaret went on to say however that she had just received the news that *Hidden Agenda* would debut at number three in the *Sunday Times* bestseller chart, which everyone was pleased about.

"So I suppose congratulations are also in order," the publicity director said, begrudgingly.

Towards the end of the meeting Sara asserted that she would like to take some of the holiday time which had long been owed to her. There was little Margaret could do to deny her request, given that she couldn't afford for her assistant to take time off between the crucial period of Sept – Dec. So she (reluctantly) allowed Sara to take two weeks off.

That afternoon Sara received an email from Adam Cooper's literary agent, Edward Carter. Both he and Adam were sorry but they would have to now cancel the publication dinner. Unfortunately they had to fly to New York on business. Sara wrote to the literary editors and other guests who had been invited to inform them the dinner was off. She also spoke to Polly, whose best friend worked for the literary agency that Edward Carter was a partner at, and asked if she could get the scoop on what was transpiring.

Polly got back to Sara within the hour with news. Adam and his agent had flown to New York to sign a US book deal. The *New York Times* had also offered Adam a position to work as a correspondent for them. The far juicier gossip, Polly wrote in the email to her colleague, was that Adam's agent had informed Martin Tweed that Adam would not be signing his next UK book deal with Bradley House. He would be signing his next deal with Richmond Books, partly to work with Richard Earle, an experienced editor there. Earle would allow Adam to write historical fiction, rather than just pigeon hole him as a military thriller author. Adam had written to Martin Tweed however to cite how happy and grateful he was for all the hard work Bradley House had put in to make *Hidden Agenda* a success. The author mentioned being particularly impressed with the enterprise and proficiency of Sara Sharpe in publicity (when Tweed summoned Julian Smythe up to his office to relay the disappointing news the editor first tried to argue that Adam had moved publishers because he had been unhappy with the publicity department, until the publishing director showed him Adam's letter which, if anything, cited Julian as the cause of his defection).

Something swelled up in Sara's stomach, and in her throat, when she read Polly's email. She dipped her head down, behind the monitor. She hoped that her features were not betraying her feelings, but she couldn't be sure. She felt a modicum of betrayal, that Adam had kept his plans to himself. He must have already made the decision to switch publishers before their tour together. Yet why should she have been entitled to know his plans? Who was she to him? And wasn't there a chance, in his mind, that she would have shown more loyalty to her publisher than to her author? And did he also know that he would be moving to New York? He hadn't said anything. Was she supposed to be his last UK conquest? Sara experienced a gut wrenching sense of loss, or finality. Bradley House would no longer want to arrange any events for an author who had left them. She would never have cause to see him again. She felt something akin to grief. Yet Sara also felt happy for Adam. She was more pleased for him than she was disappointed for Bradley House. Adam had mentioned how much he wanted to write historical fiction – but how Julian had argued that he should just stick to what they knew.

Could things have turned out any differently?

Sara had more questions than answers about the whole affair, but wasn't that the case with everyone about everything?

Move on – from Simon and him.

18.

The following day was the first day of Sara's holiday, or the first day of the rest of her life, she determined. She called her sister and arranged for them to meet for lunch. Carly was a little surprised by the call – to the point of being suspicious and worried – but by the time she put down the phone she was pleased that Sara had got in touch.

After speaking to her sister Sara logged on to *The Bookseller* and other relevant trade websites to check for editorial assistant positions – and applied for a number of jobs.

I'm worth a hundred Julian Smythes.

As well as replying to Frank Porter to arrange a date for giving a talk to his crime and thriller writing group in Birmingham Sara also emailed a few contacts she had who ran other writing groups. She offered to give a talk to their members about publishing and publicity, for gratis.

Over the next week or so Sara continued to apply for jobs. She also started researching and writing her novel, a romance set in Regency London. Jane Austen and Coleridge would make cameo appearances. The story would revolve around the character of Virginia Rake, a governess torn between her faith/duty and her love for a Byronic poet, Aaron Miller. The working title of the book was *Rake's Progress*.

Sara thought long and hard about it but decided, after a week, that she would just post a message up on her Twitter and Facebook pages to say that she had broken up with

Simon. She wanted to put things behind her and didn't want to tell everyone individually, re-living the hurt and embarrassment each time. Although Sara added that she wanted some privacy and there was no need to get in touch a couple of old friends from her modelling days insisted that they take her for a night out, to help take her mind off things. They went to a club off Bond St, wearing outfits that left little, or a lot, to the imagination. The club was full of neon, frosted glass and polished chrome – and dark corners and toilet cubicles that could house more than one occupant. Thankfully the music in the club wasn't too intrusive and they played Rick Astley as well as, heaven forefend, Usher. Instead of shouting, or merely saying "pardon" or pretending to hear, Sara was able to genuinely catch up with Kelly and Sasha, who were still in the industry. Not much had changed, in terms of both their characters and their lives. They were flirting however with the idea of leaving modelling.

"We're becoming too old and too fat," Sasha half-joked.

Fortunately they were not in the mood to spend their time flirting with guys for the night, which, unfortunately, didn't prevent various guys from trying to flirt with them. Even without comparing the would-be suitors to Adam they seemed dull and witless to Sara. One of them started to talk about how he loved Duncan Ferris, "comedy genius." Most talked about themselves, or tried to. Kelly and Sasha were proficient at blunting the arrows on Cupid's bow before they'd even been fired.

"I've been waiting for you all my life," one hair-gelled copyright lawyer said.

"Really? I've been waiting for the past three minutes for you to leave," Kelly replied.

When they were not being accosted by blokes (whose greatest love affair they'd ever have would be with themselves) Kelly and Sasha offered their old friend their support. Sara was better off without Simon, they asserted. They also conveyed how much they admired and envied Sara, for having gotten off the treadmill all those years ago and gone to university.

"You stepped off the Yellow Brick Road Sara – and found your own path. Which took a brain, a heart and courage," Sasha remarked, pleasantly surprising herself by how much she meant what she said.

"You seem sorted in regards to what you want from your career now... But do you have your eye on anyone in the romance department?" Kelly said, thinking that she could ask both her fiancé and her other boyfriend if they knew anyone suitable she could date.

"No, I don't have my eye on anyone," Sara answered. *Not unless I can buy myself a telescope that can see across to New York.*

*

During her holiday Sara kept busy (she even still kindly helped Polly out from home, so she didn't get overwhelmed with work and have *Cruella* on her back). She also tried to have fun with Rosie. They went out to the cinema and theatre – and Rosie suffered many a defeat at Scrabble in the evening in the name of their friendship.

Yet still Sara found time to frequently – and endlessly – think about the state of her heart. She thought little of

Simon (in more than one sense), but thought a lot about Adam. There was something missing from her life – and she knew it was him. It was as if the spine had been broken on her favourite hardback book, or her favourite CD had been scratched and it could no longer play properly. She scrolled down to his number on her phone a couple of times, but refrained from calling.

Sara listened to music while she worked on her novel. It helped fill the leaden silences – and also some of the songs, about loneliness, made her feel less lonely. Where once love songs had resonated and made sense (for that brief moment), now only sad songs struck the right chord. She even made a playlist and listened to it on a loop: Celine Dion, Emmy Lou Harris, Billy Joel (of course) and The Dixie Chicks. "This ain't nothing but a Heartbreak Town."

But just when Sara depressingly thought that all love songs turn into sad songs she received a phone call one morning, from an unknown number.

19.

"Hello, Sara? This is Victoria Glass."

Her voice was polite, posh and confident. Sara was so shocked she paused before replying, as if unsure of her own name and everything else.

"Yes, this is Sara."

"I was wondering if you might be free this early afternoon for a coffee. I have a window in my schedule and I'd like to meet you, if it's convenient."

Although she proposed the meeting as a request, there was something in her tone that expected that the request would be granted. Victoria Glass was used to getting what she wanted.

Sara gave her address to Victoria (who relayed it to her driver) and then asked, "Would you mind telling me why you'd like to see me Miss Glass?"

"Please, call me Victoria. And there's no need to worry, I'll tell you everything when I get there. Although I suspect that you know what, or rather who, we'll be discussing... My driver has just informed me that I should get to you within an hour or so..."

Not even Adam had made her heart beat as fast as it did right now. Confusion and anxiety twisted themselves together like rope and a knot grew in her stomach. At first Sara stood frozen to the spot, in her kitchen. It was late morning and she still wasn't even dressed yet. People didn't meet Victoria Glass wearing M&S pyjamas, especially not ones made from a blend material with a picture of Tigger on the front.

She changed quickly (changing her outfit twice), falling over whilst doing so when she couldn't get her foot into the leg of her jeans. Once dressed Sara sped downstairs and did her best to go to war on her apartment, armed with some polish, a dust buster and a bin bag. As she did so Sara asked a hundred questions and formed even more answers as to why Adam's ex-wife was coming to see her but until she arrived any speculation seemed fruitless. Her nerves eclipsed a sense of intrigue.

When the doorbell went Sara shivered, as if the noise announced the presence of the grim reaper. She took an involuntary deep breath and opened the door.

She was momentarily speechless. Victoria Glass was stunning. Nature had endowed her with a perfect figure, but she still worked-out to maintain, or improve, it. The midday sun gave an added lustre to her eyes, skin and glistening lips. Her long, glossy full-bodied black hair hung over her shoulders with precision as if she were about to audition for a shampoo commercial (and she would have got the part). Victoria Glass radiated both refinement and glamour, which is rarer than you might expect (certainly any number of footballers' wives and presenters of Strictly Come Dancing are unable to do so). Victoria was wearing a simple yet elegant Alexander McQueen belted crepe dress. The snow white outfit showed off her tan, legs and arms – without somehow being revealing. Sara suspected that Victoria Glass could still give off an air of poise and style in a potato sack though. The pair of

Christian Louboutin shoes she had on cost half the sum value of Sara's entire wardrobe. Her Bvlgari sunglasses, which she courteously took off as Sara opened the door, doubtless cost as much as the remaining half.

For a brief moment Victoria narrowed her almond-shaped eyes and took in the book publicist. Sara felt like she was being assessed, as if she was being given the once over by modelling agents again.

"Hi, thank you for seeing me at such short notice," Victoria warmly remarked, extending a finely manicured hand for Sara to shake. "Thank you James, if you want to wait back in the car I shall be half an hour or so," she then said, turning to her driver who stood by the gate.

Sara invited Victoria to come in and asked if she wanted anything to drink. She felt nervous, uneasy in her own home as if royalty were visiting.

"Just a glass of water will be fine, thank you."

Sara here felt even uneasier, realising that Rosie had finished off the last bottle of mineral water the evening before. Had Victoria Glass ever had to drink tap water?

"I'm sorry, but will tap water be okay? I'm afraid I've run out of bottled water. Usually I have plenty in."

"Tap water will be fine," her guest replied, smiling. She genuinely didn't want her surprise visit to cause any undue anxiety in her host.

There was a part of Sara that was prepared to dislike her (sort of) rival. A part of her wanted Victoria to behave haughtily and conceitedly. Sara had envisioned the scene beforehand, similar to that of when Lady Catherine de Bourgh visits Lizzie Bennett at her home, towards the end of the *Pride & Prejudice*. She imagined that, for whatever reason, Victoria Glass would look to somehow intimidate or look down on her. Yet the tabloid courtesan was being unfailingly nice, disarmingly normal.

Sara invited Victoria to sit down on a chair (her best one). She noticed how Victoria not only wore little jewellery, but she often rubbed her ring finger from where her wedding band had once been.

"You're probably wondering why I'm here," she remarked, giving Sara her third best smile – which was still more than enough to continue to melt any tension in the air.

"It had crossed my mind," Sara replied with understatement, feeling a bit more at ease in the presence of the (powerfully) attractive socialite – Adam Cooper's ex-wife.

"Partly I'm here due to a sense of curiosity. I had a long conversation with Adam over the phone last night. He's still in New York, although he flies back tomorrow. By the end of the conversation I knew that he still cared about me, but he's no longer in love with me... We've needed to have the conversation that we had last night for a long time. I tried to get through to him last week but he wasn't answering my calls... I'm not sure how much you already know but we had a whirlwind romance...Yet there was a gentleness to the relationship also. We became friends as much as lovers. At the time I had developed a burgeoning drug problem. Adam took advice from professionals, as did I, but he more than anyone helped get me clean – and I'll always be grateful to him for that. The likes of The

Priory are for people who want to get publicity, rather than get well. Drugs cost less than the fees they charge...

"For all of the passion that we shared the thing I miss most is how Adam could make me laugh... We used to spend our days together, consciously living out of the spotlight. Adam would write in the morning and then we would have lunch, go for a walk or play tennis. Or I would drag him along on a shopping trip... Occasionally I would drag him along to a party too, which he would protest about but then charm anyone he spoke to. Most of the people I know had never encountered someone genuinely intelligent and gallant before...

"We occasionally would visit his family. They're wonderful by the way, if you haven't already met them. Adam's still just a boy from South London at heart who loves his Mum and enjoys nothing more than going for a drink down the pub... He encouraged me to pursue acting. He had his writing and he wanted for me to have a similar purpose and passion in my life. I invited him to join me when I went over to Hollywood for a month but he had a deadline to meet and I knew how ill-suited he'd be to Los Angeles... I slept with a producer... It was stupid and it was wrong... Adam found out and left me..."

Victoria here took a sip of water. It was the first time that Sara thought that she might break down, when recounting her relationship with Adam. For once her pristine features appeared strained, pained.

"I used to think that people acting unfaithfully was the most natural thing in the world. Perhaps I still do. But I now know that it doesn't make it right... I was in denial when I came back to London. I tried to blame Adam, for encouraging me to pursue a career in acting and go off to Hollywood. The whole town is greased by money and sex – and they didn't want my money... I hated him for leaving me. He came back briefly, when I said that I was worried I'd return to taking drugs. I also lied and said I was pregnant... But once he knew the truth he left again... And I was angry at him again... The happiest day of my life was when Adam proposed. The saddest day of my life was when I signed my divorce papers... My agent and publicist said I needed to use my marriage, or rather divorce, as a selling point. But I cannot blame them entirely for creating the narrative that I was a wronged woman. I wanted to take things out on Adam for leaving me... I don't particularly like parts of my life at the moment Sara... In order to play the fame game – and keep the 'Victoria Glass brand in the spotlight' as my agent says – I've wrongly insinuated that Adam drank too much and was unfaithful while we were married.

"I came here today to tell you that my sins do not belong to Adam. He never cheated on me, no matter what I might have alleged in the press. He doesn't even cheat when it comes to playing Scrabble... He's the best of men, if you haven't already figured that out... Making other people happy makes him happy. What I want to say is, give him the chance to make you happy... Please don't hurt him. I've hurt him enough... Finally, one of the reasons Adam called me last night was to let me know that he was hopefully going to start seeing someone again. He asked me not to comment on any story that might come out in the press, and to stoke any fire... He values his privacy and doesn't want the tabloids door stepping you either. I want to let you know that I won't say anything. I'm also no longer going to speak to the press about Adam or my marriage..."

There were times when Sara felt that the scene was surreal, of having Victoria Glass sit in her living room and lay bare her heart. She could have taped the conversation, sold the story to *The Daily Mail* and retired. Yet Sara was too often gripped by what was being said to have time to think about the strangeness of it all. She also couldn't help but like the witty, dazzling yet vulnerable woman. In another world they might have even become friends, she speculated afterwards. Adam has good taste in women it seems, she wryly thought to herself. Victoria still clearly missed him. In some ways, Sara believed, she loved him more now than when they had been married. But it was over. She'd eroded his trust and admiration. Victoria Glass was now in a state of mourning for Adam, rather than deluding herself that she could bring their relationship back to life.

One of the reasons why Victoria had desired to meet Sara, that she was less forthright about, was that she wanted to divine Sara's feelings for Adam. And what was it about the publicist that had captured his heart? But when she went fishing for answers Sara didn't bite. But how could Sara articulate her feelings for Adam when she had yet to fully understand them herself? She remained coy about the state of her relationship, or non-relationship.

Victoria stayed for forty-five minutes, but then she heard her driver sound the horn outside. She again thanked Sara for seeing her on such short notice – and then apologised that she had to leave so abruptly. But she had an important meeting to attend across town. She needed to help re-design the shape of the bottle for her perfume.

20.

Sara slowly walked back into the living room after Victoria Glass' car pulled away. She slumped down on the sofa. She was in a state of shock, as though someone had just told her that she'd just won the lottery or that two plus two really equalled five. The afternoon sun shone through the window but Sara still felt in the dark. There were still more questions than answers. Her head – and heart – were fit to bursting after hearing what her unexpected guest had to say. She struggled to take everything in.

Shortly after Victoria left Sara opened an email from Polly. She mentioned how Victoria Glass' PA had called her and asked for Sara's number. Polly also said how she had just checked her Facebook and was sorry to hear the news that Sara had broken up with her boyfriend.

When Rosie returned home from her work Sara finally got the chance to pour her feelings out, along with pouring out a large glass of wine. Rosie sat open-mouthed, popping a Malteser into it every now and then, as her flatmate told her about her day. Rosie looked on in awe and disbelief almost at the chair that Victoria Glass had sat in, imagining perhaps that she was still present. She could still smell her criminally expensive perfume. She was even tempted to pitch a story to her editor, "Victoria Glass Comes To Clapham", but rightly thought better of it.

After being somewhat dumbfounded by her friend's eventful afternoon Rosie did provide some potential answers to questions Sara had.

"How comes he hasn't told me about how he feels?" Sara asked, wrinkling up her face and squeezing her hands into two small fists in frustration and confusion.

"From what you've said it seems that he's quite old-fashioned. Maybe he wants to speak to you face to face."

"But it's now been well over a week since I've last heard from him. What's changed?"

Sara here came up with an answer to her own question. Around a fortnight ago she had set up a Facebook and Twitter page for her author – programming things so that he could follow her pages and news too. Had Adam checked his feeds and discovered that Sara was single again?

"The question you should really be asking yourself is not how comes things have changed, but what are you going now to do about? Do you like him?"

"He could be the best thing that ever, or never, happens to me Rosie... He makes me feel that anything is possible... I'm not sure if I would be applying for jobs, writing a novel or getting in touch with Carly again without him... I can't sleep properly, thinking about what could happen between us and what I might have missed out on... But the person I want to get close to is three thousand miles away... Adam knows everyone. Nigh on everyone he meets likes him. But I know he's lonely. He needs someone and I want to be that someone, who kisses the tears away... He saw and did things in Afghanistan that still haunt him, I think... This is not just about giving him a chance. It's about giving me, us, a chance... We're forever reading magazine articles or watching TV programmes telling us how important money and sex are... Adam reminds me of how important friendship and decency are... And in being sweet I think he's as sexy as hell, or chocolate... But what do you think?" Sara finally asked her friend, drawing breath and reaching for the last but one Malteser in the box.

"I think that every time you say his name your face lights up. And sooner or later you're going to have to find someone else to play Scrabble with, because I'm getting tired of you beating me all the time. I also think you should invite him over as quickly as you can, while the flat still looks as tidy as it does. But most of all Sara you shouldn't be telling me about how you feel. Tell him about it!"

And she did.

21.

Two weeks later.

Morning. Petals of golden sunlight sparkled all across Lake Windermere. Gleaming white sailboats glided over the cool blue water beneath a serene, cloudless sky. Rich greens and browns, from the trees and grasslands, framed the landscape.

Sara soaked up the picturesque scene outside her hotel window. The birdsong from the balcony had woken her. She breathed in the scent of wildflowers and sighed in pleasure, or rather contentment.

The only thing between them now was the material of her silk pyjamas as Sara lay next to a sleeping Adam, her leg entwined with his beneath the covers. They had a day planned, of sailing, visiting Dove Cottage and buying presents for friends and family. Sara already knew what she wanted to buy her sister and her imminent niece or nephew. But Sara wanted nothing more now that to just stay in bed with the man she loved.

Yes, loved.

*

The morning after Sara's unexpected encounter with Victoria Glass she had been determined to speak to Adam. To tell him how she felt. Sara called Polly to find out from her contact at Adam's literary agency when he was due to fly in from New York. Before Polly could get back to Sara however Adam had called her from Heathrow. He had been nervous, but equally determined to speak to her. Adam had asked if Sara was free to meet that afternoon.

They met in Battersea Park, by the bandstand. Adam asked if Sara would like to take a turn around the park. They walked and talked. Adam explained how he had not kept in touch because he had recently been the victim of infidelity – and did not wish to be the cause of it also. He said that she seemed to be happy with her boyfriend, when she spoke about him when they were on tour. Sara replied that, if she seemed happy, it was because she was with him rather than thinking about Simon. By the end of their first circuit of the park they were holding hands.

It was only after reading the message which had come up on his author's Facebook page that Adam had dared to hope. Sara here told Adam about his visit from his ex-wife, which he had been unaware of. On another day Adam would have been upset with Victoria for interfering, but he realised that she may have acted as an unwitting, or witting, matchmaker. Besides, Victoria was his past. He had the future to look forward to, with *her*.

"But what about New York?"

"I'm moving back to London. There was always something missing in my life there."

"What was it?"

"You... How about we both try and make a leap of faith – and catch each other?"

By the end of their second circuit of the park they were kissing.

*

Sara rested her palm on Adam's bare chest as he slept, and she snuggled up to him. She smiled, as if sharing a joke with herself, as she realised that their heartbeats were in sync.

Sometimes sad songs turn in to love songs.

Part of her wanted to wake him up, hear his voice, kiss him, caress him and make love. But he looked so content sleeping that she let him rest. They had been up late last night – not playing Scrabble. She reached over to the bedside table and switched on her iPad, which was sitting on top of her copy of *Lyrical Ballads*.

She checked her messages. She had just been sent her first batch of submissions, which she would need to read over before starting her new job as an editorial assistant at Falcon Publications next month. Polly had sent her an email to say that she had arranged her leaving drinks for next Friday. Sara received an email from Charlotte Hurst congratulating her on her new job. Charlotte added that she knew that Sara had it in her to flourish, which meant a lot to the soon to be editorial assistant. After dropping the bombshell that she was leaving Bradley House even Margaret Duvall called her into her office and wished Sara well, in as sincere and heartfelt manner as the gnarled publicity director could manage. Mercifully (for both of them) the exit interview didn't last too long, as *Cruella* was dying for a cigarette at the time. Julian Smythe was nowhere to be seen on the day that Sara announced she was leaving. He had been called into a long meeting with Martin Tweed, for some unofficial re-training. Her sister sent her a quick message to say that she and her husband Gordon were fine with the proposed date for her and Adam to come around for supper.

"I've just seen a picture of him online and read one of his books. He's a keeper. If you let him go though, I'll have him. Gordon won't mind, or even notice..."

Sara's final email was from Rosie, who said she and Eddie would make sure they'd come along to her leaving drinks. Having been inspired by Sara telling a man about how she felt – and the said man not running a mile – she asked her friend to fix her up on a date with Eddie Woolly. Their night out was a success. They clicked. Already Rosie was having a good effect on Eddie, Sara fancied. He had shaved off his beard and he was even using the Kindle that Rosie had bought him as a thank you for taking her to dinner and the theatre. She wanted to see a musical, rather than Ibsen, next time they went out to the West End though.

Adam began to stir. Sara put the iPad back on the table. Work and everything else could wait.

"Morning. Look at the beautiful view," Sara said, pointing out of the window.

"I am," he replied, not taking his eyes off her – cherishing her.

Adam drew Sara close and kissed her. She held him, whilst letting go of herself. She breathed in his scent.

He tastes even better than Maltesers.

"I thought we might have breakfast in bed," Sara proposed, after finally coming up for air. "How do you feel about muffins to start off the day with?"

"They're not really my thing."

Well, nobody's perfect.

Printed in Great Britain
by Amazon